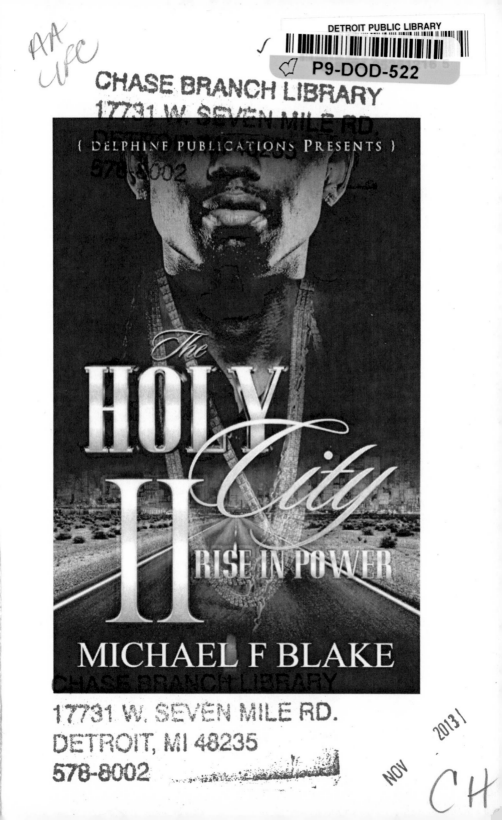

(DELPHINE PUBLICATIONS PRESENTS)

The HOLY City

II

RISE IN POWER

MICHAEL F BLAKE

Published by Delphine Publications

Delphine Publications focuses on bringing a reality check to the genre urban literature. All stories are a work of fi ction from the authors and are not meant to depict, portray, or represent any particular person Names, characters, places, and incidents are either the product of the author's imagination or are used fi ctitiously, and any resemblances to an actual person living or dead are entirely coincidental

ISBN: 978-0989090681

Edited by: Tee Marshall
Layout: Write On Promotions
Cover Design: Odd Ball Designs
Printed in the United States of America

Dedication

In loving memory of Herbert Lewis Turner who has lose his battle with cancer. You will forever be in our hearts. Love you Cuz!

Acknowledgements

First and foremost I would like to give God all praise for everything he has done for my life. He turned a person who never took reading and writing serious in school into an author of a published series; MAN, that can't be nothing but God! Thank you Lord for enhancing my gift of writing. I will forever be indebted. I'm nothing without You!

I would like to thank my mother, Kelly Blake, for her unwavering support. You are definitely one person I can always count on. I love your business sense; it keeps me on my toes! You have been there with me through EVERYTHING. Words can't express what you mean to me. There's no way I could pay you back, but my plan is to make you proud of me and to show you that you are appreciated. Thank You, Ma!

I would like to give a heartfelt thank you to my long time friend that recently became my wife, MarQueta LaToya Blake. You made this writing transition very easy for me when I was incarcerated. Looking at pictures of you and my son and re-reading every letter you sent helped me write with no worries. Knowing that I was coming home to a secure home and someone that had my back throughout all the hardships was a blessing and that's what I consider you--- a true blessing from God. Love you babes!

I also want to thank my little entrepreneur in the making my son, Michael "Mikey" Blake J.r. You are an amazing kid! I see nothing but a bright future for you. Thanks for all your unexpected great ideas. LOL! I learned that sometimes if you just listen to half of the things your kid(s) says some of it will actually make a lot of sense. Love you Da!

Last but not least, I would like to thank my host of Aunts, Uncles, and Cousins who supports me and do everything they can to raise awareness to my literary brand. Thank you! Love you all!!!

In closing I would like to shout out the Lawndale Community and the entire West side of Chicago for producing historical events and people that allowed me to create such an incredible story. There's a "Holy City" in every major 'hood in America. If we, as a community, don't learn how to confront the problem realistically, then drugs and crime will continue to destroy our inner city youths.

The

Holy

City

II RISE IN POWER

PROLOGUE

Since the massacres of Peanut and Spoonie, the Holy City had changed dramatically. Everyone in the IVL Nation understood that high ranked officials had sanctioned the killings. Spoonie was considered a snake in most people's eyes, but the status he held within the organization made him a loved man amongst a majority of the Lords from 21st. The two bodies were never discovered for a funeral. The Nation had no problem finding closure for the fallen five star elite; everyone knew it was family business. Even with that said, some IVL affiliates who were extremely loyal to Spoonie tried to rebel against Chief Marcus. After a few outlandish shootouts involving Lil G, Peewee, and other close members from Marcus's mob, the loose cannons were later found murdered outside the neighborhood. The abnormal war between the Lords of 21st and Marcus was quickly stemmed. The soldiers who made it out alive came to their senses and immediately became obedient; following suit under Marcus's command.

Marcus badly wanted to appoint one of his personal partners to replace the vacant slot that Spoonie once held, instead he had no other choice but to appoint Ricardo Smith aka Rico, the five star elite Supreme for the Insanes. Rico was from outside of the Holy City and had been putting in a lot of work throughout the years. He had been involved with the Nation for most of his childhood life.

As a youngster, Smitty took a real liking to Rico's loyalty to the Nation and the respect he demanded amongst his peers. When Rico was only a juvenile, he caught kidnapping and attempt murder charges during a mission for the mob. After serving a 10-year bid in some of the toughest penitentiaries Illinois had to offer, Smitty allowed him to control the neighborhood where he was raised.

Rico had very interesting traits. He had the features of a black man but his short, natural wet, wavy hair and pecan complexion gave away his Puerto Rican descent. His 5'4" stature was far from intimidating. Although Rico was a fairly short guy, he had very big shoes to fill.

There hadn't been any major problems going on within the mob over the past couple of years. The only confusion was the constant miscommunication between Marcus and Smitty. Marcus was the man who called all the shots on the streets. When it came time to make major decisions for the Nation as a whole he would confer with the committee, which consisted of Big C and other originals. Smitty was still labeled as the Chief of Chiefs over the IVL's while in the joint, but a lot of things were going on in the streets that he had little control over. Marcus kept a phone line open for Smitty to call and made sure he lived like a kingpin. They barely had phone conversations, messages usually came to Marcus indirectly. Smitty couldn't deny the ambition Marcus conveyed to uplift the Nation financially, but were there some issues he disagreed with that had come about?

Two years had passed since the shootings that nearly took the lives of Marcus and Peewee. They both recovered and continued to roam the streets as if nothing had happened. Marcus blessed Peewee with three star elite status and let him control all the blocks that surrounded the Holy City area. Lil G got the head of security position. In other words, when Marcus was ready to send out a hit squad, it was up to Lil G to take care of the situation accordingly. J.R. and Marlin continued to play their roles. Although they all started out as equal counterparts, they all understood why Marcus elected Peewee to be a made man. Once the streets became knowledgeable of Peewee surviving after nine gunshots it put a certain sense of fear in a lot of people's hearts and they looked at him as somebody not to be fucked with. Peewee and Lil G together was definitely a force to be reckoned with.

These days Marcus rarely had to get his hands dirty with any hands-on murders or drug deals. The only exception was when it came time to re-up on supplies. Kunta, the Nigerian connect, never wanted to meet with anyone other than Marcus. From the time Shawn introduced the two, their business relationship blossomed. Shortly after Marcus's near death experience, the spot on Division that he and Shawn operated diminished and was taken over by the Four Corner Hustlas in that area. Before fleeing town, Shawn even paid the fifty thousand dollars that B-lo demanded and turned over the remainder of the supplies. Once Marcus healed from his gunshot wounds, he owed Kunta over two hundred thousand.

Kunta understood the predicament Marcus was put in and allowed him enough time to pay the debt. After learning about Shawn's disappearance, Kunta lost all respect for him and cut off all connections with him and his uncles. Marcus was now Kunta's new golden boy. He made sure Marcus stayed supplied with bricks of cocaine and keys of the best heroin in Chicago. There was no question,

Marcus was the supplier for everyone in his mob and a couple of other VL branches. It was virtually impossible for other affiliates to go elsewhere to get work due to the low prices, high potency and consistency that Marcus produced.

While Marcus was healing, someone unexpectedly came into the picture to help him recover; that person was Peaches. Peaches was the ride or die type of chick that every street hustler needs. She was there by his bedside until he got well enough to do things on his own. She was there to do all the dirty work; from changing blood stained bandages all the way down to changing his urinal bag.

When Marcus healed well enough to have sex, he ended up getting Peaches pregnant with a baby boy. Even though Peaches had three kids of her own, she never second-guessed having Marcus's child. Due to his success level, Peaches knew he would take good care of his child and her other three.

Marcus did keep it real with Peaches by setting her up with a car and three-bedroom bungalow home in Bellwood, a suburb 20 minutes west of the city. He even connected Peaches with a nice paying job through one of his legitimate friends who held a high position at a particular banking and loan corporation.

Marcus's reign as Chief helped him accumulate major cash, enough for him to have an extravagant home built from the ground up. Like most kingpins, the house was located far out from the city. Marcus took advice from Kunta and moved into a neighborhood not too far from his estate. After dropping a light three hundred thousand on an all brick, two level, five bedroom, three-car garage monument, Marcus included all the necessary add-ons to make it a dream home. Including an indoor/outdoor swimming pool, a blacktop basketball half-court, and a mini-gym with a built in steam room and Jacuzzi.

It took a lot of convincing from Marcus to get Sylvia, his beloved mother, to move out of their long time rented apartment and move her and his younger brother, Chris, two hours outside of the inner city. Once Marcus assured her that everything was legal and under control, she eased up and made the extravagant house a comfortable home.

Marcus purchased the two flat apartment building where they once lived and transformed it into a duplex. It became one of his stash houses and trick off spots. He felt secure in the area because everyone on the block was immune to his street status and had love for him since his childhood years. This was just one of several locations that Marcus had around the city. Marcus moved around unpredictably. He made it virtually impossible for anyone to pinpoint his whereabouts.

On the outside looking in, it seemed as though Marcus had it all, but when it was all said and done, there was still a personal matter he kept bottled up inside of him for many years...his father's murder! Marcus accepted Steve as a father figure but there was no replacing his real dad. He still had an urgent longing to find closure. Would the truth of his fathers' unsolved murder ever be revealed or would it remain an open chapter in Marcus's book of lifeforever?

Chapter

1

After blowing the loud whistle several times to get his players' attention, Coach Woodward stopped everyone in their tracks to scold Chris after a lackluster suicide drill attempt.

"Christopher...!" He yelled. "...Don't think for one minute that you don't have to put forth an effort while running these drills! The last two trips down you were the second to last to finish; that's unacceptable from my point guards. Keep that up and you'll find yourself spending most of your time next to me this season!"

Chris sucked air between his teeth before lowly mumbling, "Get the fuck outta' here." No one except his teammate that stood directly next to him along the baseline was able to hear his verbal comeback.

"Don't let 'em get to you, dawg. You kno' coach jus' be talkin' shit." Randy, his fellow teammate and best friend, whispered as they all caught their breath and waited for further instructions.

"All right! Everyone get in their groups so we can run a scrimmage. Now, I need to see hard nose defense being played and a lot of hustle. If by any means I don't get that, my whistle will be blown and everyone will report back to the line for suicides. Do I make myself clear gentlemen?!" Coach Woodward asked in a serious manner.

"Yeessssss!!!" A team of fifteen, tired teenagers dreadfully roared back.

Coach Woodward was known for chastising his players. Years back, he was involved in a scandal for physically abusing some of his players that would talk back or miss practice. All of that ended after he put his hands on the wrong student. One day after practice, one particular student must've had enough of his physical and verbal abuse and gathered up his street friends to pay Coach Woodward a visit. A gang of young thugs met him and they beat him relentlessly. He suffered a concussion, two broken arms, and a fractured rib cage. That was a good enough message for him to keep his hands off other people's children.

With all that said, Coach Woodward was a great coach. He had a system that couldn't be denied and had led the Bulldogs to four city championships and one state title. Because of Coach Woodward, the Westinghouse Warriors were known as a powerhouse basketball academy that produced many college players; some even made it as far as the NBA or overseas.

While exiting the gymnasium doors, Chris and his teammates made it outside to see the sun setting on a breezy October evening. It was the beginning of the school year and autumn was definitely in effect. Around this time of the year, the sun began to set early and the streets were usually dull by nightfall.

Chris was now a junior in high school and had obtained a license to drive. As soon as he got his license he begged Marcus and his dad to buy him a car to commute from the south suburbs, where their house was located, to the city to attend school.

Of course they agreed under certain conditions. They made Chris agree to bring home passing grades, gave him a curfew, and made him promise to stay focused on his craft, which was none other than basketball. Staying focused on basketball wasn't Chris's problem, but the schoolwork was. Chris soon fixed that problem by hiring a group of intelligent female classmates to not only complete his assignments but also help him study when it came down to exams. They had no problem working with the star player.

Every day after leaving school or practices, Chris would always drop his two friends, Dante and Randy, off at home. The car that Chris was flaunting

3

around the city was fancy for someone of his age. Marcus bought him a turquoise '95 four door Buick Regal. The car was sparkling clean with 19 inch chrome rims, windows lightly tinted, and a bangin' sound system; A typical street hustler type of car. Chris didn't mind being looked upon as a hustler. They were the most respected in the 'hood.

Everyone began to scatter and go their separate ways. It was obvious the other players admired Chris's car as they watched the three of them approach the Regal. None of the other players were fortunate enough to have an older brother or even a father figure to buy them a vehicle. Most of them didn't have fathers in their household and if they had older brothers, they were usually small time street punks or dope fiends.

"Watch out man! You kno' it's my turn to ride shotgun. I let'chu' ride in the front all last week!" Randy and Dante shoved back and forth over who was going to ride in the passenger seat.

"Y'all niggas need to chill. Actin' all thirsty over who gon' ride in'a front; fuck around –n- make both y'all walk." Chris snapped as he popped the locks with a press of a button. They both settled down and Randy ended up getting the front seat action. After starting the car, Chris flipped through his book of CD's and pulled out Juveniles' latest album, 400 Degreez. Chris was inserting the disc in his JVC detachable face face off CD player when Randy pulled out something that grabbed his attention.

"Look what I got." Randy grinned as he pulled out a dime sack of mid-grade weed from his pocket and scanned it by his nose.

"Nigga, what'chu' waitin' on! Roll that shit up!" Dante exclaimed from the backseat, showing definite signs of anxiousness to smoke.

"I would if I had some'nt to roll it up in, dumb ass...!" Randy smartly replied. The two of them stayed at each other necks but still were the closest of friends. "...Aey Chris, stop up there at that Citgo so I can get' a White Owl to roll this," Randy insisted.

"Man look, y'all know I gotta be at the crib by nine o'clock," Chris looked down at his Movado wristwatch. "It's already 6:30."

"Okay, you got two and a half hours before you have to be in the house, what'chu' trippin' on?" Dante sarcastically stated.

"I'm sayin, it takes me an hour to get to the crib and I need to get there on time," Chris quickly shot back.

"Well guess what, you ain't gotta smoke. Stop and get me a blunt so I can get high by my damn self," Randy said.

"Yeah you'a luv that." Chris retorted jokingly as he quickly scanned through the CD player, going directly to track nine, one of his favorite songs on the

400 Degreez album. "...See me I eat, sleep, shit, and talk rap. You see 'dat '98 Mercedes on TV I bought 'dat..." Were the lyrics heard banging from his trunk that held two twelve inch woofers with the proper amps to push out the sounds.

Accelerating out of the school's parking lot, Chris reached toward the backseat to grab his all black White Sox fitted cap and carefully placed it on his head, giving it a slight tilt to the left. From that point, they were on their way to having a good smoking session while joyriding through different blocks on the West Side.

Chris had a lot of freedom at the tender age of sixteen, but at the same time, he knew his boundaries and what lines not to cross. Marcus knew about Chris's growing weed habit, he would even smoke with his younger brother on occasion. Marcus felt the weed wasn't having a negative effect on Chris behavior. He still handled his business on and off the court and was able to cover it up to where Sylvia wouldn't suspect anything.

Clearly, Chris was the best player on Westinghouse team and arguably the most popular student in the school. As a freshman, he was number one in scoring and assists amongst all high school players in the city. By his sophomore year, he led the Warriors to a city championship and a trip down state only to lose in the sectionals. All of the newspapers predicted Westinghouse to be the state champions for the upcoming season and Chris was ranked as the top point guard in the city. So it was safe to say thatChris was living the life that most teenage athletes in the 'hood would die for!

Marcus sat with Big C and Steve at an old antique soul food restaurant called Fellowship that was located on the corner of Kedzie and Ogden. This wasn't an ideal fancy and remodeled spot that's always packed with customers nor did they offer the best soul food around. This was merely a place where the three of them often conducted business in their own private section. Despite a few older faithful customers, this place was usually empty or closed. Big C had family ties with the owners since the days of his father, so he was entitled to do pretty much whatever he wanted around the joint.

As they nibbled on the food in front of them, majority of their talk was reminiscing on old times and of course business, legal and illegal.

"Look at'chu..." Big C began to say while looking at Marcus in likes of a proud uncle. "...I remember when you was a snotty nose kid running 'round here. Now you sitting in the highest seat for one of the most high-powered mobs in the city...You kno' I'm proud of you, right?"

Marcus simply nodded his head in agreement with a slight smirk as he gave Big C his undivided attention.

"Hell, you even allowed me to fall back and now you handlin' all my business; you done come a long way, boa'," Big C continued.

"Well, you kno', y'all been puttin' work for years. Sooner or later it comes a time when the torch has to be passed down," Marcus stated in a respectable manner.

"Yeah, I'm jus' glad it was passed down to a righteous man..." Big C said before taking a sip of water. "...Now, I'm sure you know this shit ain't about to get any easier. You got niggas out here plotting as we speak. You got these crackers waitin' on the smallest slip up so they can lock yo' ass away forever. So, therefore, you need to have an exit plan...I mean you always goanna be who you are, but just make it out in one piece and wit' somethin'."

Steve sat there in silence during Marcus and Big C's conversation. Steve and Marcus indulged in these types of talks on a daily basis. Marcus listened to Big C's advice, but for some reason he felt there was something behind all of this and sure enough he was right.

"Now I didn't ask you to come up here jus' so I could talk ya' ear off wit' this lecture bullshit," Big C mentioned.

"It's all good, good advice is always helpful," Marcus claimed.

Big C hesitated before stating, "I have a small dilemma."

"Talk to me." Marcus replied with a more attentive expression.

"I what'nt gon' approach you wit' it and jus' let Psycho handle it for me, but I don't need these detectives runnin' 'round here wit'a open murder case."

Once he mentioned Psycho's name, Marcus knew it was some dirty work that needed to be done. Psycho was a Lord from off 16th street that Big C allowed to be in charge over a portion of the Conservatives in that area.

"It's this ball playin' ass nigga from out South been owing me about forty stacks goin' on two months now. He's really not a threat, but'chu' know how I feel about niggas who play games. I go by his house and they lie for 'em, making it like they ain't seen him. I call his phone and he never answers it. He really was jus' an ole friend I was tryna' put back in 'da game and this the thanks I get." Big C said, shaking his head in disappointment.

With no hesitation Marcus simply asked, "What'chu' want done to 'em? You want me to grab

10

'em and get'cho' money or you want him brought to you?"

"Well, you know the money ain't really an issue..." Before Big C could finish his statement, the waitress from behind the counter came over.

"Excuse me, I don't mean to interrupt, but was you guys expecting anyone?"

"Yeah, yeah let 'em in," Marcus assertively replied.

As the waitress politely strolled away, Marcus turned his attention back towards Big C and Steve. "It ain't nobody but Lil G and Peewee. I told them to meet me up here."

"Like I was sayin', money ain't a problem you know that; I jus' want a clean disappearance." Big C stated with a stale expression.

Lil G and Peewee walked up. Peewee held a Finish Line apparel bag with a shoebox inside.

"Whudd up, Lord." Peewee greeted as he handed Marcus the bag. While speaking all at once, he and Lil G acknowledged Big C and Steve accordingly.

"You want us to wait outside while y'all finish talkin'?" Lil G asked respectfully.

"Nah, I was waitin' to catch a ride wit' you," Marcus said while pulling back from the old wooden table.

11

"Lil G," Steve began to state. "...you ain't knocked anybody off today, have you?" He jokingly chuckled.

"Nawl, not yet, Unk... but'chu' kno' the day still kinda' young!" Lil G laughed while glancing down at his watch as the three of them headed for the back exit.

"Awe yeah, I almost forgot," Marcus slowed down and turned back toward the table. "This is for you." He said as he tossed the Finish Line bag to Big C.

Big C took a peek inside the shoebox and gave Marcus a nod of approval along with a smile after seeing nothing but clean fifties and one hundred dollar bills wrapped in rubber bands.

"Don't spend it all in one place." Marcus quoted, obviously trying to be funny. Out of nowhere Steve blurted out, "Where my bag at!" His statement made them all laugh, then he continued to say, "...You ain't been out to the house all week; you know yo' momma been worried."

"I'a be out there this weekend. And tell her to quit worrying herself so much."

"You know how ya' momma is, man," Steve said to end their back and forth exchange.

As Marcus and his crew left out the restaurant, Big C had nothing but great things to say about Marcus. He always commended Marcus's hustling ways and loved how he ran his mob with an iron fist. Big C even put Marcus in control of all operations concerning his branch of VL's. All he asked of Marcus was a generous monthly check. Big C was still labeled as the King over the Conservatives and also had his own members in place, but they all had to report Marcus for their supplies.

At the young age of 24, Marcus had a lot on his plate and was handling it like a seasoned veteran in the game.

Chapter 3

It was an abnormally warm 70-degree day in October. Everything seemed to be going at its normal pace on 21st and Trumbull.

A normal day consisted of customers rapidly coming back and forth to purchase rocks and blows, shorty Lords running wild if they weren't working packs or jabs, as they called them. This particular day, one of the Lords by the name of Nutso decided he was going to work all the jabs for the day and no one was going to tell him anything different. Nutso earned his street name respectfully. He was one of the older Lords who was never wrapped too tight from the start. Throughout his thirty some odd years of being alive at least fifteen of them had been spent back and forth behind prison walls. When Nutso was younger he was known as a go getta' but as time passed by, his respect level was slowly declining and the shorties were quick to let it be known.

While walking down Trumbull kicking up dust, two shorties named Lil Reesie and Midnight were becoming frustrated with not being in the pack rotation during the morning dope rush.

"Who the fuck this nigga think he is?" Lil Reesie complained. As Lil Reesie and Midnight walked to the other side of the street, they witnessedNutso serving a few customers. "...It's goin' on five o'clock and he still workin' all the jabs?! I bet'chu' 'Wee didn't give him the green light to do that shit."

"You know how that nigga Nutso is man. He think he be run-in' shit when Peewee or Lil G ain't around," Midnight added, edging the situation on.

"Fuck that, I ain't goin'! He gon' have to let somebody else work or I'm gon' shut all this shit down!" Lil Reesie said as they both started to cross the street.

Lil Reesie was sixteen going on thirty. He was one of them young 'monkey niggas' that was sure to grow up to be a 'guerrilla' if guided correctly. Lil Reesie was still growing into his adult frame but his mouth and the way he went about things showed nothing less than a full-grown thug. Midnight, on the other hand, was still a bit young minded and timid at times. In other words, he knew who to fuck with and who not to fuck with.

15

"Aey Lord, lemme' holla' at'chu'?" Reesie chanted as he inched closer to the other side of the street where Nutso was stationed.

"What the fuck you want wit' me 'lil nigga? Don't you see I'm handlin' grown folk shit?" Nutso exclaimed with aggression as he looked at them both before serving a long time, loyal customer. Nutso knowingly disrespected the shorties and started making small talk with the anxious hype.

"I'm saying', you ain't gon' let nobody else work?!" Lil Reesie questioned confidently.

"Work what...?!" Nutso shot back quickly, giving the shorty his attention with a murderous expression. "...I'm runnin' shit on this block from now on! That's why shit so fucked up ova' here now, you lil young stupid mothafuckas don't know how to hustle. All y'all wanna' do is make enough' money to buy some weed wit' and that's it." He said all this while counting the money from his recent sales.

The customer felt the aggression building in the air and eased off.

"Man, Jo, ain't nobody tryna' hear 'dat shit. I know damn well Peewee ain't told you to work the block all muthafuckin' day!" Lil Reesie stated loudly while showing different hand gestures to get his point across, displaying no signs of fear in his young soul.

"Listen boa', you or nobody else cain't tell me shit about no block on this strip! I been out here befo' any of you niggas!"

"And outta' all 'dem years you still ain't got shit! Nigga, you's a nobody to me!" Lil Reesie fiercely shot back as the commotion began to rise.

Nutso looked as though he had enough of the youngster's gibberish. He folded the cash that he was counting and tucked it in his pocket before saying, "You betta' get somewhere befo' yo' mouth get'chu' in some'nt yo' ass cain't handle." Nutso calmly stated with a point of a finger in acts of giving out a warning. Midnight, who had been quiet throughout the entire altercation, stepped in and said, "C'mon Reesie, lets ride..." He stood in front of Lil Reesie and started back peddling him away from the scene after seeing the seriousness in Nutso eyes. "...It's moving slow ova' here anyway."

"Pussy ass nigga, I can handle anything come my way!" Lil Reesie continued his reckless talk as Midnight backed him toward the end of the block. "...Fuck 'dat nigga, man! I murk niggas like him!" He said before turning the corner, loud enough for Nutso could hear him.

Nutso stood there with a cold stare on his face and quietly stated to himself, "Alright...okay," while walking off nodding his head.

17

Chapter
4

Sitting in his platinum blue, custom Cadillac Escalade sitting on 24-inch Lowenharts, Marcus and Rico conversed on different issues concerning the areas where the IVL's dwelled. These two had a mutual understanding with each other and they damn sure were respected amongst the Nation as upright leaders. Marcus was more groomed and conducted himself with class as his money grew. Rico was still considered a 'hood star and showed his power through force and intimidation. Rico always dealt with Marcus on a personal level when it came to getting his supplies to avoid any mishaps. Marcus knew Rico honored him for being the active Chief but was well aware of his unconditional love for Smitty; Rico was always going to view Smitty as the ultimate leader of the mob despite his imprisonment.

"So what's been goin' on over there off Cicero? Y'all been straight over there?" Marcus asked with concern as he passed Rico a blunt filled with some of the finest weed the city had to offer.

"Yeah, you kno', everything been copasetic. A few incidents here and there but nuttin' too major." Rico replied while inhaling the weed smoke.

Marcus was parked on his old block, 19th and Hamlin. They continued to smoke and Rico, the five star branch elite, made sure to fill Marcus in on all the matters involving Nation business throughout the city.

"Yeah, I jus' recently sent a crew of Lords out south in the Wild Hunits to claim some land that was owed to us. I'ma 'bout to flood the area wit' work so we can grow and expand even more..." Rico put emphasis and authority on every word. "I what'nt gon' tell you until we got shit established but fuck it, now you know."

Marcus never minded expanding the Nation's territories but it seemed as though Rico was taking matters into his own hands. Instead of making a big issue out of the situation, Marcus agreed with the move and proceeded to take care of business.

"Aight then, lemme' know when you got it together. I'a ride through there and check shit out," Marcus said.

"No doubt, no doubt. It won't be long, especially wit' that dope you been givin' us lately. I know 'dem mothafuckas gon' come runnin'." Rico stated with a high expression as they both shared a brief chuckle.

After a few seconds of humor, Marcus quickly got back to the situation at hand.

"I got'cho' normal package plus five more of 'dem thangs like you asked. Everything ready for you back there in the trunk of that blue Delta Eighty-eight sitting in the middle of the block." Marcus confirmed while handing Rico the keys and pointing in the direction of the car through his rearview.

Before exiting the truck, Rico suddenly changed the topic and caught Marcus off guard.

"Awe yeah, you ain't heard from Smitty?" Rico bluntly asked as he turned from pulling the door handle all the way.

"Yeah, I try to holler at 'em at least once a week. Why, wassup?" Marcus countered with suspicion growing in his eyes. In all actuality, Marcus hadn't talked to Smitty in months.

"Jus' checkin'. I been thinking about Chief lately and was wondering how he was doin'. You kno', I sho'll miss..." Rico's statement was cut short due to the ringing of Marcus's phone.

"Hold up a minute, Lord..." Marcus said while turning his attention to the caller ID of his Nextel. "...Hello?"

"Hey You!" An excited, sexy female voice came through the receiver.

"What's goin' on?" Marcus tiredly responded back.

"You tell me; are we still on for lunch or what?"

"We could do some'nt."

After sensing Marcus deeply getting involved into the phone conversation, Rico hand signaled his departure. Marcus stopped him in his tracks.

"Hold on for a second, Nicole..." Marcus sat the phone onto his lap. "You straight?" He asked.

"Fa'sho," Rico assured him.

"Aight, hit my phone once you make it to where you goin'."

"I got'chu'. ALMIGHTY!" Rico chanted as he aggressively tapped his chest with a fist before throwing up the VL sign.

"MIGHTY!" Marcus repeated the same gesture, matching Rico's aggression. To say 'Almighty' was another way the VL Nation acknowledged and greeted one another.

To prevent having encounters with different members affiliated with the mob, Marcus supplied Rico with the appropriate amount of work to distribute to different elites within the Nation. The normal monthly package for Rico was forty bricks of pure cocaine and ten keys of excellent heroin. Marcus was getting such a good price that it allowed enough space for Rico and the other elites to make a nice profit off each piece they gave out on consignment. Kunta was giving Marcus sixty bricks of cocaine at a time for twelve-five apiece and thirty keys of raw heroin for forty thousand each; everything was issued to Marcus on consignment on a monthly basis. Marcus would then give his people a brick of coke for fifteen thousand and a key of dope for sixty-five.

It was virtually impossible for any hustler in the streets to get these low prices. Therefore, other elites were able to break all their supplies down into grams and ounces to quadruple their profits. Every month Marcus would usually profit around nine hundred thousand, give or take; street value for everything, unimaginable! Marcus had majority of the West Side on lock. If you were getting any type of real money in the streets, Marcus was usually the reason why.

Lil G and Peewee waited patiently in an all-black 'Crown Vic' with dark tint that made it impossible to see their faces clearly. They stationed themselves on an unfamiliar block located on 71st and Normal, the South Side. A blue Astro Van filled with young Lords was parked directly across the street from them. They were all in position for the mission they were appointed to. The favor Big C asked of Marcus was in motion.

"This nigga must've relocated or some shit," Lil G began to point out. "We been sittin' out here for damn near two hours and I ain't seen no signs of dude comin' to this crib yet!"

"We gon' wait a lil' while longer. If this nigga ain't pulled up in thirty minutes, we up. But no matter what, this ma'fucka gotta' go. Even if we have to post up ova' here the whole week!" Peewee spoke out in his best O'Dawg impersonation from Menace II Society.

Marcus had two of his main enforcers and three thorough young soldiers to assist them on this particular mission. Once Marcus got all the adequate information he needed, he made a move on his own time without telling Big C anything. Marcus felt no need to inform him until the situation was handled.

Twenty minutes after Lil G made his statement, they began to feel uneasy and started to pull out of the parking space. They weren't able to put the car in drive good before the entire ordeal made a three-sixty turn.

"Holl'up, holl'up," Peewee said while eagerly looking in the rearview, stopping Lil G from pulling off. "That ain't the car we been waitin' on is it?!" Peewee instantly prepared himself by revealing his pistol and cocking it. That was a good enough sign for Lil G to get back into position.

Within seconds, a white CLK 320 Benz coupe slowly began pulling up in front of the two-flat building they had been scoping out for the past couple of hours. After identifying their target, Lil G gave the Lords in the Astro Van 'the eye', giving them the green light to go ahead with the plan. Before the Benz settled into park, two of the Lords were innocently easing their way towards the target.

Not knowing what was in store for him, he got out to approach a first floor apartment without any suspicion.

24

"Excuse me, sir, you kno' where building 7110 at?" One of the Lords asked while the other faked a phone conversation on his cell phone as they both gradually got closer.

"What!" He disgustingly replied as he glanced up from fidgeting with a hand full of keys.

"Does a girl name Renae stay in yo' building?" Shorty asked semi-respectably.

"Look dude, I ain't got time to be givin' out information. I got bin'nis to attend to," he claimed in an impatient tone as he continued with his task.

"My bad, sir. I didn't mean any harm." Everything shorty said from that point on was disregarded. By his head being down and focused on his situation, he never expected any problems. In the matter of seconds, his entire understanding changed.

As soon as Shorty slid his cell phone onto the clip attached to his waistline, out came the all black steel. Within two steps, he was in point blank range of his victim.

"Yeah mothafucka, you kno' what time it is," Shorty said in a low-pitched tone with the pistol directed towards their adversary's midsection.

"What the fuck!!!" He instinctively jerked back with fear. "You little crazy mothafuckas! I told y'all I don't know no damn Renae!" He nervously pleaded with his hands up, looking down at the pistol pointed towards his stomach. In the midst of the standoff, the other Lord signaled for assistance.

"I don't know 'dat bitch either, but'chu' comin' wit' us tho'."

"Look man, if y'all want some money go in my pocket and get what you want and let me gone 'bout my bin'nis." Before finishing his statement the blue Astro Van swerved up burning rubber with the side door slid wide open.

"I ain't getting' in that ma'fuckin' van! Y'all niggas gon' have to-"

BLOCKA! In mid-sentence, a shot sounded off that tore through the kneecap of the victim.

As he hysterically cried out for God and anyone else he thought could possibly save him, the Lords successfully dragged him inside the van and sped off with Peewee and Lil G leading the way. They proceeded toward their disclosed destination, which was a construction site located on the border of Indiana and East Chicago.

During the 20-minute trip to the low-key industrial area, the young Lords did everything from pistol-whipping to duct tapping, and tying their victim up with rope. Once making it to the location, the young Lords forcefully straddled their badly beaten victim from the van to meet up with their counterparts. The entire view was filled with sewers, mountains of dirt, mud, and rocks. Even after being shot and beaten their victim continued to put forth a struggle. As he wiggled and mumbled distorted screams, the young Lords dropped him directly in front of Lil G and Peewee.

"Bitch azz nigga; don't cry now." Peewee stated with a crazed expression on his face. He stood in front of the victim and forcefully snatched the gray duct tape from his mouth. After letting out several painful screams, he began to plead for his life.

"Why y'all doing this," he cried out. "If it's about some money I'll take you to where everything at! Just don't kill me man, please!!! Please!!! Don't kill me!" After spilling the beans to every spot where he held his valuables, Lil G finally broke the news.

"Thanks for all the tips, but that ain't what the fuck we came for," Lil G said while the helpless victim was in the middle of pleading for his life. "I'm sure you familiar wit' the name Big C?"

The pleas calmed down for a split second. The expression forming on his face showed a sure sign of death.

"That's what this about?" He pitifully retorted while grimacing with extreme pain. "I can take you to get a hunit' thousand right now! That's way more than what I owe Chief! I'm tellin' y'all, we could work this out!" He helplessly stated, trying any antic that could keep him alive.

"Unfortunately, that ain't what he wants," Peewee said irritably as if he grew tired of the grown man cries. With a simple nod of the head, Peewee

27

instructed the young Lords to carry on with the mission. Instead of shooting him and making a scene, they had something much more brutal in mind. Next to them was a sewer with the top pried off. After covering his mouth again with the duct tape, Peewee ordered the Lords to hang him by his ankles and drop him head first into the never ending sewer. While holding him in the air, dude squirmed and wiggled like a fish caught on a hook as he saw death right before his eyes. After about thirty seconds of holding him in the air and watching him panic and lose control of his bowels, Peewee simply pointed downward and in an instant, the person was no more. The sewer was so deep, it was impossible to hear or see the body hit the bottom. One of the young Lords slid the top back onto the sewer as if nothing happened. Lil G and Peewee unremorsefully shook up with the other Lords and agreed on a meeting spot back at the headquarters.

Lil G and Peewee took it upon themselves to hit all the locations the victim confessed to stashing valuables. This was a move they didn't have to report back to Marcus, it was looked upon as an incentive that comes out of the line of duty.

Chapter
6

During his relaxing ride to the extravagant home, where he rarely stayed, Marcus smoked while contemplating on many situations concerning him and his crew. This crib was mainly built for his mother and other immediate family members. Whenever there were family functions more than likely it was hosted by Sylvia at the house. When relatives came over to visit on special occasions, the house was a sight for them to see, being that majority of the Williams family were still living in poverty throughout the inner city. Although Marcus helped out most times, it was never good enough for certain family members.

The hour and a half stretch from the I-290 expressway to the city's far south suburb come to an end once he exited at 183rd Street which led him to Cicero Road. Cicero was one of few main roads that ran from the West Side through to the far south.

As he pulled up to the circular driveway in his everyday car, a '97 money green Cadillac STS,

Marcus noticed that everyone was home from all the cars being parked in the drive way. Stepping out the car Marcus took a brief moment to look around at the mansion in amazement, obviously reminiscing on the road it took for him to gain success. He finally stepped foot inside of his home only to smell the aroma of a gourmet breakfast being prepared.

I came at the right time, didn't I?! Marcus thought excitedly to himself after seeing his mother in the kitchen over the stove on a beautiful Saturday morning. Marcus kicked off his shoes before walking on the plush white mink carpet that rested on the living room floor and crept up behind his mother.

"Ooooh, boy! You scared the living shit outta' me!" Sylvia exclaimed, reacting to Marcus discrete embrace. He then kissed her on the check and said, "Maaaa, what'chu so scared of? It's jus' me," Marcus pecked her on the cheek once again. "I told you 'bout worrying ya'self so much. You need to relax."

"How can I relax when you won't let me?" Sylvia said, showing signs of nervousness.

"What'chu mean I won't let'chu?"

"Hell, it's been two weeks since I last saw you, Marcus. I don't be knowing if you dead or alive."

As Marcus nibbled on a strip of turkey bacon straight out the grease he replied. "That's what I mean, Ma... you can't be worried 'bout things we cain't control. We gotta' put everything in God hands and jus' roll wit' the punches."

30

Without being able to argue the fact Sylvia retorted, "Whateva', but I know one damn thing, you bet not stick them nasty ass hands back in my food. Wash ya' hands and fix you'a plate like a normal human being." Sylvia playfully scolded her first born.

Marcus took heed to Sylvia's motherly demands. It wasn't long before Chris darted down the steps after hearing his brother voice in the house.

"I knew I heard you down here. Long time no see fat boa'," Chris teased while watching Marcus pile his plate with scrambled eggs, hash browns and pancakes. "What brought you this way?"

"What'chu' mean?" Marcus questioned with a confused look. "I live here, nigga!" Marcus finished his statement with a mouth full of food.

"Hey, hey, watcha' mouths!" Sylvia interfered with the friendly bickering.

"Yo' son gon' make me beat'em up," Marcus claimed while stuffing his face with food.

"Yeah, you'a luv 'dat!" Chris responded humorously while making his way over to the food.

"I don't care if y'all kill each other jus' don't do it around me," Sylvia said in the midst of them going back and forth.

"STEVE! Come on down and eat before the food gets cold, honey!" She shouted while putting the final touches on the food.

31

These were the loving times that the Williams family were missing out of their lives as of late. Sylvia believed the house was going to bring more togetherness, but it was the other way around. Having a license to drive kept Chris out and about, Marcus had several other spots to lay his head, and Steve was still active amongst the Nation. When times were presented for them all to be together everything was genuine.

At times Sylvia felt uneasy while at home by herself. Mostly because she knew what type of life her son and husband led outside of their home.

While eating breakfast, everyone enjoyed one another and rambled on about things that occupied their daily lives. It wasn't long before Chris hit his brother up for some money and claimed he had to be somewhere and jetted out the door. Before Marcus was able to do the same, he was idled by Steve.

"Marcus, befo' you get up outta' here let me spit a bug in ya' ear."

Before he could continue Sylvia said, "Look at'chu', ain't been here a whole hour and you already about to run yo' ass out the door. Ain't gon' take a shower, change clothes or nothin', huh?"

"Momma, I ain't goin' nowhere," Marcus stressed while giving a helping hand with removing the plates from the glass table.

"I got' a headache and I ain't had no good rest in' a 'boutta week."

32

"I'll take care of these," she said sincerely while taking the dishes out of his hands. "You go 'head and get you some rest, baby."

Marcus kissed his mother on the forehead and headed toward the steps, on his way towards the five bedrooms. After seeing Steve out back shooting shots on their half court blacktop , Marcus had no intentions on getting any sleep. He basically put on a front for Sylvia. As soon as Marcus stepped foot on the court he immediately ran underneath the basket for a rebound. After a shot taken by Steve hit nothing but the bottom of the net, Marcus got the ball and began a little trash talking.

"You cain't play ball no'mo, ole man!" Marcus taunted as he awkwardly dribbled through his legs three times then took a long range shot that surprisingly hit off the fiberglass backboard.

"I bet'chu' five hunit you cain't hit that shot again!" Steve said with a grin as he passed the ball back to Marcus.

"Bet! Bet!" He anxiously said as he performed the same dribbling move, but this time losing control of the ball. After chasing the rock down, he concentrated on making his next shot. As soon as he released, Steve hollered out, "That's off!" Sure enough he was right; Marcus shot a brick so hard it nearly took down the backboard.

"...Lemme get that," Steve blurted out excitedly as he palmed the ball with his left hand and held the other one out to collect.

"As long as I owe you, you'a never go broke." Marcus laughed, hitting Steve with the old saying.

"Don't worry 'bout it I kno' how to get it up out'chu'!" Steve jokingly shot back. They laughed off the friendly bet and Steve continued to shoot around, knocking down majority of his shots without touching the rim. While Steve shot jumpers, Marcus got the rebounds.

"What's goin' on? You need to holla' at me 'bout somen't?"

"Awe, yeah," Steve said while cautiously peeking inside to see Sylvia's whereabouts. "I set up a trip to the Bahamas so me and ya' momma could getaway for about a week." With a sense of relief Marcus replied, "Maaan, Lord knows she need'a vacation."

"I'm letting you know now because I want it to be a surprise. Now, I kno' ya' brotha' think he grown, but keep a tab on'em while we gone."

"You know I'ma do that anyway; so when y'all leaving'?"

"Next Thursday; we gonna' stay to the following Thursday."

"That's wassup," Marcus said as they shook up and bumped shoulders. "I need to take me a vacation soon'a later."

While they continued to converse, Marcus received an interesting phone call. As the vibrator of his Nextel alerted, Marcus couldn't help but to take the phone off the clip and checked the caller I.D. Once noticing the number he answered without any hesitation

"You couldn't of called at a betta' time," Marcus said through the chirp of his Nextel.

"What's going on my brotha'?!" Kunta replied, trying to speak clear English.

"Ain't nuttin' to it; out here by the house takin' care of a few thangs...what's on ya' mind, Jo?" Marcus asked.

"JO...?" Kunta questioned jokingly. "Who the hell is Jo?"

"You understand what the hell I'm saying'."

Kunta laughed and said, "I can't comprehend that street jive shit you talk!"

As the two of them went back and forth across the Nextel walkie-talkie, Steve patiently stood there and listened. He was well aware of the position Kunta played in Marcus's life. He knew Kunta was the reason Marcus had access to whatever drug he wanted in its purest form. For a young guy, having a loyal and honest connect like Kunta was a rarity. Marcus never took his situation for granted; he showed his loyalty by making Kunta an honorary family member. In fact, he even invited Kunta and his wife over for dinner at the house several times to meet his family. That made Marcus more trustworthy and accessible to getting whatever he needed.

After a couple minutes of small talk and laughing at each other comments, Kunta resumed on a more serious note.

"Listen, since you already out this way, why don't you take a ride with me. I would like to present some things to you."

"Come'on now Koont," Marcus said with a long drag. "I promised my ole girl I what'nt goin' anywhere so soon. She ain't seen my face in'a couple weeks and you kno' how she be worried about me since that shit happened."

"Yeah, I kno', I kno', but it's something you need to see for your own good," Kunta attracted Marcus's attention with his last statement. "Trust me, I'll have you back in no time."

After a slight pause, Marcus chirped back, "Aight man, but'chu' have to pick me up 'cause I don't feel like driving."

"No problem...I'll be pulling up shortly." Kunta said in a smooth, slick tone.

Once ending the conversation, Marcus and Steve both looked at each other with confused expressions. They couldn't help but wonder to what Kunta had in store to show Marcus.

36

Chapter 7

Kunta mentioned nothing about where they were headed when he picked Marcus up. Marcus figured it couldn't be too serious and if it was he was ready for whatever. He knew it wasn't a special occasion because of the type of car Kunta was driving.

"Outta' all your cars, you come pick me up in this piece of shit. Wassup wit' that?!" Marcus blurted out humorously. The two door Lincoln Mark VIII was actually in mint condition and drove pretty smoothly. A normal working class person would've been proud to drive this type of car, but for Kunta, this was far from his Mercedes Benz and Porsche collection.

Smiling and letting out a light chuckle Kunta replied, "We don't have to ride luxury all the time. You have to stay under the radar sometimes in your life."

"I know that's why I drive my STS most of the time," Marcus stated.

"A fucking Cadillac...!" Kunta exclaimed in his normal loud tone. "And you call that staying under the radar?" Kunta shook his head in disbelief.

"Anyway, where the hell you taking me? We been driving on this same road for about thirty minutes!" Marcus claimed while glancing at his wrist watch.

"Chill Marcus, Chill...! Ain't I your brotha?" Marcus turned his head and let out a long sigh before answering, "Yeah."

"Okay then, you have nothing to worry about." Kunta assured him in a low raspy tone with a puzzling glare in his bloodshot eyes.

After an hour drive, Kunta finally pulled up to an old, humongous factory that looked as if it had been there forever. The front of the warehouse read, M&K Carpeting Distributor in big bold letters. The area was very discreet and it seemed that the warehouse was the only building on the narrow street. There were no surrounding houses or any neighborhoods within a mile or two radius. Kunta drove the full length of the warehouse until arriving in front of silver plated, barbed wire gate that had a 'private property' sign posted. He pressed a button on the gate and stated a code name through the intercom. After a few seconds, the gates slowly slid open.

As they drove into the parking lot, Marcus noticed several semi-trucks with the company name, a few civilian cars, and a bunch of loading docks with semi-trucks backed into them. Kunta settled into a parking space that blended in with the rest of the cars. Marcus didn't ask any questions and was being very observant of his surroundings during most of the ride, but once he exited the vehicle, he broke all silence.

"So you brought me all the way out here to buy some gaddamn carpet?!" Marcus asked sarcastically as they were approaching the main dock that lead to an entrance.

"Hell no...!" Kunta replied, "This is one of several businesses that I own. Come'on let me show you around. I promise you it won't take too much of your time."

Marcus reluctantly walked alongside Kunta towards the warehouse. He knew Kunta was a businessman and had other things going on besides the drug business, but never did he take time to explore the other side of him.

When they entered the warehouse, they saw normal and productive workplace activities in progress. There were forklifts moving large rolls of carpet from one side to the other, a busy customer service section, and trucks were being loaded and unloaded left and right.

Instantly, Marcus noticed that all of the workers favored Kunta, in other words, they were all of Nigerian descent. Everyone was working hard and focused on their assignments. Once the workers became aware of Kunta's presence, they were all smiles and honorable greetings. One of the workers, who seemed to be in control over operations, acknowledged Kunta with a handshake and a hug before walking off a few steps ahead of Marcus. While Marcus stood there observing the scene, he experienced a few welcoming nods, warm smiles, and even some unpleasant stares from the other workers.

After afew moments of talking and giving instructions, Kunta turned his attention back to Marcus.

"Marcus, come; I want you to meet someone," Kunta said as he caught Marcus in a slight daze. As Marcus walked towards the two men, Kunta introduced Marcus to the person he was conversing with.

"Marcus, this is Jude; the man that makes sure everything runs smoothly around here." After shaking hands and greeting each other, Jude spoke out, "Marcus, I hear a lot of great things about you; very good man." He said in a foreign accent. Kunta proceeded to give Marcus a brief tour around the warehouse. In the middle of walking and explaining to Marcus how the business worked he introduced him to the rest of the staff.

As they continued to walk and chat, Marcus couldn't help but feel the pressure of Jude shadowing their every move. Marcus thought nothing of it and kept on with the tour guide. Marcus respected Kunta for taking time out to show him around one of his places of business, but his mind wondered what was the sudden cause for the tour.

Kunta finally ended the tour of his carpet factory and was now prepared to talk other business with Marcus.

"Now, I know you're wondering what this was all for?" Kunta questioned while leading Marcus to what looked like his private office space.

"I mean, it's cool to know the person I'm dealing wit' is one of the top carpet distributors in Illinois, but if you thinkin' this is somen't I'a be interested in, well I don't know about all that."

"Well Marcus, one day I hope that you would be interested in building your own legitimate empire besides the one you have in the streets..." Kunta explained as he opened the office door allowing Marcus to enter first.

"Fortunately, showing carpet was not the primary reason I brought you here."

The office space was congested with carpet scraps and the extremely tall walls were covered with different styles of carpeting and insulation.

"Have a seat," Kunta insisted while pulling out a seat in front of a desk that was crowded with different types of forms and papers. With Jude following them into the office, Marcus's awareness grew, "Now I know we've been doing business for a few years now and things have been going exceptionally well..." Kunta stated after resting in the seat behind the desk, "Marcus, as you already know, you are like family to me. I really look at you like a younger brother." Marcus sat there nodding his attentively, wondering where the conversation was headed.

"So with that said, it's only right for me to assure you that our business will continue to prosper for more years to come." As soon as Kunta finished his statement, he gave a slight nod of approval to his head man in charge. Jude walked over to what looked like a security system and after pressing a ton of buttons, two of the walls began to slowly open. In a matter of seconds, Marcus witnessed something extraordinary. As he moved his head from side to side , then up to the almost never ending ceiling, he saw more drugs than he had ever been around in his entire life, in his dreams , or T.V. for that matter! Kunta literally had bricks of cocaine and kilos of heroin stacked as tall as skyscrapers!

Marcus was in complete awe. His eyes widened and his mouth dropped as if he was in a room surrounded by pure gold.

"Marcus, Marcus...you alright over there?" Kunta asked. A stunned Marcus shook his head. "Believe me, it's more where this came from, but like I told you when I first laid my eyes on you, when it's over, it's over. What you see is what you get; all of this was meant for you and only you. This is enough supply to set, not only us, but our families straight for life...!" Kunta exclaimed with an aggressive whisper as he continued, "As I said from the start, all I ask for is loyalty and you have been extremely loyal; that's why I call you my brother. Unfortunately, I can't say that for everyone." Kunta finished his statement by making eye contact with Jude. The silent order obviously was meant for Jude to secure the room because with a push of a few buttons, within seconds, everything was back to normal; there was no sign of drugs or drug paraphernalia anywhere in sight.

Marcus sat there speechless and just when he thought he had seen it all, Kunta was ready to bring something else to his attention.

"Marcus, I have one more thing to show you. Come, follow me," Kunta said as he rose from his seat. He opened a door behind him that led to another room that was connected to his office. This area was much different. The moment Marcus stepped foot inside he felt the temperature drop to damn near freezing. He also noticed three separate vaults made out of pure steel and opening the door was like turning a knob to a safe.

With Marcus still being in a state of shock, the three of them stood in front of one the walk through vaults.

"Marcus, when I call someone my brother or family, I mean it from the heart. I would go through the ranks for that person, but when he disrespects me in any way or make me look foolish, let's just say I take that quite personal." Kunta explained forcefully, obviously sounding as if he was trying to get a certain point across. Not needing further instructions Jude took it upon himself to unlock the vault.

When the squeaking heavy metal door slowly opened, Marcus didn't expect to see what was set before his eyes. In front of him hung a deceased, naked body frozen up like an icicle. The person had been brutally disfigured and was barely recognizable. Once Marcus zoomed in closer on the face, he saw features of his old childhood friend and past business associate, Shawn!

Marcus stood there controlling the mixed emotions that electrified his soul. He didn't know whether to feel angered or be relieved by the situation. For the past two years Marcus had contemplated killing Shawn if he ever caught up with him. When Marcus was ambushed and left for dead, Shawn disappeared and was nowhere to be found.

44

He even left Marcus thousands of dollars in debt with Kunta and left behind the gold mine operation they had worked so hard to build from the ground up. Over time, Marcus was able to pay the debt off and continued success with Kunta. Marcus never forgot how Shawn betrayed him, but as time passed and the more money he started getting made him less focused on the matter. Kunta never brought it to Marcus's attention that he wanted Shawn dead, however, his actions showed otherwise.

"Now Marcus, I know this is a hard pill for you to swallow. Believe me, I hated to do this. I don't like doing business this way," Kunta explained nonchalantly while the three of them stood in front of the dangling body. "But it had to be done. Not only was he disloyal, but he also betrayed you as a friend and left you for dead!" He expressed his anger in a devilish tone.

Marcus was speechless. Although there were mixed emotions going on inside, he still managed to look Kunta directly in his bloodshot eyes without showing any emotion or fear. Before leaving the room, Kunta ordered Jude to dispose of the body using their language.

There was little conversation between the two on the gray and cloudy trip back home. Not one time did Marcus mention the excitement, followed by the horror he witnessed. Marcus sat on the passenger side with rambling thoughts. He respected Kunta as a powerful and smart businessman, but now it was time for him to respect his gangsta. Kunta had proven to him, if necessary, he had the money and the power to send for you by any means.

Before Marcus exited the car Kunta stated, "Marcus, I hope this episode won't affect our relationship."

Marcus looked him square in the eye and replied, "Why should it? One thing I do know, that shit you jus' showed me could happen to anybody, ANYBODY..." Marcus emphasized the word 'anybody' before reaching for the door handle. "I'm about to get me some rest, I'a holla at'chu' later."

Marcus entered his home, went directly up to his master bedroom, turned his phone off, and passed out. He slept for the remainder of that day. His only thoughts were of the events that had occurred earlier.

Chapter

8

"Man Jo, I cain't believe it's this nice out here and its damn near November!" Marlin said while standing amongst Lil G, Peewee, and a few other Lords. They all stood on Homan in the middle of the block drinking out of plastic cups filled with Hennessey.

"Yeah, butchu' kno' it ain't gon be like this for long," Lil G reminded.

"You gaddamn right," one of the Lords burst out after taking a sip from his cup. "I cain't wait to it get cold; that's when I do my best hustling. When that hawk comes out it separate the men from the boys, ya feel me."

On a Friday, in late October, it was an abnormal seventy degree evening. The sun was setting and it was only moments before nightfall. By the brown and orange leaves that covered most of the sidewalk, it was obvious that the changing of seasons was in full effect and winter was well on its way. The block was filled to capacity, as usual. Everyone from small children running wild, Shorty

Lords working packs, dope fiends pacing up and down the block were out. You even had grandmothers and other older people who rarely came outside, sitting out on their porches enjoying the last of the good weather before the blistering winter came aboard.

Homan was one of many blocks that Marcus's personal crew controlled. Even though the three of them stood out on Homan drinking and smoking, enjoying the last of the endearing warm days, each of them had their own sections in the Holy City to govern.

While they were talking and reminiscing with each other, they were constantly approached by every shorty that crossed their path. Some of the Lords played around with the ones they became more acquainted with on that level and others seized their opportunity to get up with Peewee on some real block issues. There was one shorty in particular who briefly caught everyone's attention as he walked up in a rapid pace to embrace the circle.

"Was' sup Lord!" Lil Reesie boguarded his way through the bunch to personally show love to his everyday leader, Peewee. He then shook up with Lil G and Marlin. After speaking his peace to the three of them, he purposely ignored the others that were standing around and proceeded to speedily walk off like he was on a mission.

"Damn Reesie, 'dem the only ma'fucka's you see!?" One of the Lords spoke out, obviously feeling himself from the few cups of Henn he had gulped down. He was an older Lord that didn't hold rank in the mob. Most of the shorties in the neighborhood had established a 'talk shit' relationship with him; but if he didn't kick it with a person on that level, he damn sure wasn't with the game playing.

"I'ont acknowledge lames!" Lil Reesie shot back with his back turned while still speed walking.

The older Lord swiftly took off chasing after Reesie. That quickly came to a halt after a splash of liquor spilled out his cup.

"...You gon' make'a nigga fuck yo' lil young ass up!!!" He hollered down the block.

"That's if you ever catch me, pussy!!! Hahaaaaaaa!!!" Lil Reesie loudly taunted while back peddling towards 21st.

"That's a'ight, you gotta' come back to 'da block befo' the night out!"

"That 'lil mothafucka somen't else," Lil G said in a light spirited tone amongst the entertained crowd.

"I heard he been terrorizing these niggas on 21st," Marlin mentioned.

"Yeah, I like Shorty. He'a kill somen't too," Peewee retorted on a more serious note.

"These niggas don't won't it wit Reesie," one of the Lords said. "'Dey kno' shorty ain't gon play no games wit'em and he don't give'a fuck who it is. They say him and 'dat crazy ass nigga Nutso got into it a couple weeks ago."

"I heard."

"I what'nt out here but they say Reesie snapped out!"

"Reesie betta' keep his eyes open. 'Dat fool Nutso ain't wrapped too tight." Peewee seriously warned before jumping to a different conversation with the others that surrounded him.

Thirty minutes had passed and the sun had gone completely out of sight. It was still early, but the short winter hours had brought on nightfall pretty quickly. The only light on the block came from the few light poles that worked. The block was still crowded and more people came around as the minutes ticked. Everyone was talking and joking with each other, contemplating their next move on a busy Friday night. Out of nowhere a loud bang sounded off, temporarily grabbing everyone's attention. It was not followed by rapid shots so they all returned back to what they were doing.

Not even a minute later, a young girl's roaring scream caught everyone's attention. After seeing a concerned pack racing down 21st to an obvious scene, everyone standing in the middle of Homan immediately followed suit to where the commotion was coming from.

At the end of the alley way between Homan and the next block over, Trumbull, lay a struggling Lil Reesie. He had both hands covering his throat and excessive blood was leaking from a wound that couldn't be seen. His mouth was wide open as he choked on his own blood and desperately tried to catch a breath.

"...Somebody call the ambulance!!!"

"...Give'em mouth to mouth!!!"

"...Lord please don't let this child die!!!" All sorts of frantic comments and suggestions were loudly blurted out amongst the frenzied crowd of people. Everyone did what they could to keep Reesie alive.

Ten minutes later, loud sirens from several fire trucks and ambulances flooded the premises. After clearing a way to the victim, the paramedics rushed Reesie onto a stretcher and proceeded to place him in the back of the ambulance. While most residents out there were hoping for the best, the Lords that stood in the crowd knew it was a wrap after noticing Reesie's leg movement slowly shutting down and a wet spot forming in his crotch area.

Walking inside of Fantastic Cutz barbershop, Marcus felt the need to spend quality time with his younger brother. Only a few days had passed since the murder on the 21st strip and of course the barbershop was the place that held all the gossip that went on around the surrounding blocks. Chris was very familiar with the shop; every week he set up appointments to get a haircut. Marcus, on the other hand, usually went when the shop was closed. The owner had no problem with it, being that they grew up knowing each other. Being labeled a Chief in a very high crime area caused for certain precautions in order to stay alive.

"Aey Marcus, I see you got the young superstar witchu!" One of the three barbers exclaimed as the two of them settled into the shop.

"Chris, whudd up!" His routine barber acknowledged. "I ain't never saw y'all two come in together, what's the occasion?" He joked.

"We jus' out-n-about and I decided to get a lil touch up, ya feel me." Chris responded in a clever fashion.

Marcus and Chris headed straight to the back where the pool table was located. While Chris waited on his turn to get a cut, he and Marcus played a couple games and of course, there was plenty of trash talking between the two. Despite the barbershop being half packed this late afternoon, the attention and conversations kept coming their way from the barbers and the few regulars that felt they knew them.

"Aey Chris, don't y'all have a game coming up?" One barber asked in the middle of cutting hair, while other conversations on different topics were in progress.

"Yeah, the Thanksgiving tournament; the first game this weekend."

"Who y'all playing?"

"Crane, I think."

"Awe hell yeah, I know it's gon be a lot of hoes up there," he said excitedly. "How many you gon' drop, 'bout thirty, forty points?"

"I'ont kno', depends on how I feel, ya' dig?" Chris replied, causing a few laughs.

Chris' popularity was through the roof in its own way. He ranked number one among all high school basketball players in the city and number three nationwide. Chris' name and face stayed posted in the Chicago Sun-Times for the phenomenal plays that he performed on the court. Anyone in the city that followed sports knew all about Christopher Williams. Everyone in the 'hood had high expectations for Chris's basketball career. Even though Marcus humbly downplayed Chris's skills when they're together, he too expected nothing but great success to come from his brother.

In the middle of their pool game, the owner, who also was a barber, asked, "Aye Marcus, did they ever find out who murk'd shorty ova' there on 21st?"

Marcus concentrated on his aim and replied, "Not that I know of." In all actuality the Lords had an idea, but Marcus didn't bother to speak on it.

"Man, that's fucked up how 'dey did shorty. I knew'em too; he was 'a cool lil dude."

"I heard somebody jus' walked up on'em and blasted him dead in the face, execution style!" One barber blurted out while shaking his head with disbelief.

"You never kno' man, shorty was into so much shit anybody could've did it. All I'm sayin' is how ain't nobody see the shit when 21st was packed wit' mothafuckas?" A bystander stated.

"I was jus' on my way over there too. Some'nt told me to change my mind," another person announced.

The entire time was filled with speculations and rumors from sideliners until the subject finally changed.

By the time Chris got in the chair, Marcus was stepping in and out of the barbershop, constantly meeting up with people he had expected to show up. When the brothers caught on to him being in the neighborhood, they pulled up by the carloads just to speak and pay their respect. Marcus's status was prominent and it wasn't often that he was posted for a long period of time in one spot. The Lords that didn't see him on a regular basis took advantage of this time with their Chief. Although everyone that stopped through showed nothing but love, Marcus made one call and had security all around him in case of any mishaps.

Marcus was talking amongst the people that stood around when his phone rang. After seeing who it was he took a few steps back from the crowd and answered it, "Yeah, wassup?"

"Where you at?" A female voice rudely blurted out.

"What the fuck you mean where I'm at. Wassup!" he grunted irritably.

"I been calling yo' phone all fuckin' week! Why you been ignoring me?" The boisterous voice on the phone was his baby's mother, Peaches.

"I been busy," Marcus replied nonchalantly.

"Busy! All week, Marcus?! Don't gimme that shit!"

"Man look, I ain't got time for this. What the fuck do you want?"

"It's a damn shame I gotta' fuckin beg yo' ass to come get'cho own son. If it what'nt for yo' momma you probably would never even be around him!" Peaches harshly stated in her 'baby momma drama' tone.

"Look Shalonda," he put emphasis on her government name, "I jus came through there and dropped off some money so-" His statement was rudely interrupted in midsentence.

"...Money ain't everything! You need to start spending time wit'cho' son!"

Marcus had had enough with the back and forth arguing and ended the call without proper forewarning. This led to excessive calling and angry voice messages from an infuriated Peaches. Marcus knew half of her frustration was coming from him not being intimately involved with her lately. Marcus's class of women had elevated since becoming a boss. Peaches hadslipped to the bottom of the totem pole. Once Chris stepped out of the barbershop door, Marcus gave his farewells to his people that were standing around before hopping into his platinum blue Escalade. While burning rubber out of the parking space, Marcus turned his music on blast and left the crowd bobbing their heads in excitement.

Not knowing where they were headed, Chris simply sat back and enjoyed the nice, luxury ride through the streets. Marcus continued to ignore the stalking calls from Peaches that were rapidly invading his cell. He decided to take a ride to the suburbs to see his son without giving Peaches a warning.

The fifteen minute drive to Bellwood ended once he pulled in front of the bungalow home that he had purchased for Peaches. Marcus never wanted all access to her home just because he lent a helping hand. He did it strictly as a gift and assurance for his son's safety.

After getting out of the truck to approach the house, Marcus knocked and rang the doorbell recklessly before Peaches finally hollered out, "Who is it!!!"

"Open the damn doe!"

"Don't be ringing' my fuckin' doe' bell like you crazy." She stated to herself, but she was still heard. Peaches opened the door and quickly turned to walk away without acknowledging Marcus at all, not knowing Chris was with him. Chris couldn't help but to stare at Peaches fleshy, plump ass jiggle every which way in her extra tight, turquoise boy shorts as she angrily stomped back towards her bedroom.

Seconds later, little MJ came running out of his room.

"Daddy! Daddy! Daddy!" He chanted innocently, running head first into Marcus's arms.

"Heeeey man! How daddy's lil soulja doing?"

"F-i-n-e."

"You see who I got wit' me, don't you?"

"...Yeeess, 'dat my uncle Chris," he said excitedly in his baby tone of voice as he jumped from Marcus arms to his uncles.

While Chris played baby games with his nephew, Marcus eased his way to the bedroom. As soon as he slammed the door behind him out came the built up rage from both parties.

"Was sup lil homey? You missed yo' uncle?" Chris playfully asked his nephew while holding him in one arm and tickling him with the other.

"Yeeessss!" he wildly responded.

With the vociferous arguing roaring from behind closed doors, Chris took it upon himself to distract his nephew from the confusion.

"Hey man, you wanna go to the store? I'ma let'chu' get what'eva you want," Chris said, making the offer sound intriguing. Not needing anymore convincing, MJ rushed towards the door and lead the way out.

Behind closed doors Peaches was in the middle of pleading her case.

"Marcus you be on that bullshit, man!" She exclaimed emotionally. "You don't even try to be in my baby life!

"Look, don't give me that shit!" Marcus shot back, showing different hand gestures to get his point across.

"Outta' all people I expect you to understand why I can't have him wit' me like that!" He barked out, making references on how dangerous his status in the streets could get at times.

"What'eva!" She dramatically replied, showing no understanding to his situation. "...You always making up fuckin' excuses." She said before flopping down on the edge of her queen size bed.

It was obvious that Peaches was venting and had issues on her mind other than what they were bickering over. Peaches' love for Marcus had deepened over the years. Even when she tried to hate him it would never last long. Marcus had a certain charm she and most ladies couldn't resist. The longer Marcus remained in her presence, it seemed as though light shined down on the mood in the room.

After being gone all of ten minutes, Chris and MJ made their way back to the house. The moment they stepped foot in the door, the noise from the bedroom went from rage to the sounds of angry, lustful sex! After hearing the extremely loud erotic pleas coming from Peaches and Marcus's explicit comebacks, Chris immediately occupied MJ's attention by escalating the volume to the television and allowing him to eat up as much candy as possible.

Twenty minutes later, Peaches and Marcus came straggling out the room, looking as if a huge burden had been lifted off their shoulders. Peaches' attire had changed from boy shorts to loose pajama pants. Her curvaceous hips and luscious backside were still very noticeable with every strut. Her attitude drastically took a turn for the better; she even came out apologizing to Chris for not greeting him at the door.

Marcus made it clear that he was taking his son with him. After briskly making MJ's bag and handing Marcus all the proper materials he needed, Peaches escorted them to the door. From that point on, Peaches felt free to do whatever she pleased now that she was temporarily free from all four of her kids.

At the well anticipated Westinghouse Warriors opening game, the intense crowd consisted of wild teens, parents, and fans of high school basketball. They all packed the Proviso West gymnasium at the first game of the annual Thanksgiving tournament. Most of the fans were there to cheer on Chris and his Warriors, who were ranked number one in the city. Their opponents were an unranked team that looked to be fans themselves from how they watched and allowed the Warriors to blow past them.   The half-time score was 52 to 28 and the crowd knew the other team's chances of rallying back were slim to none.   Most of the crowd stayed around for the second half hoping to see Chris embarrass a defender with his infamous 'killer cross-over' move that had been effective on every defense he encountered.   There were times where Chris would actually make a defender lose balance and trip over their own feet.   The phrase people used for that scene was called 'breakin ankles'.   Although Chris was short, standing at only 5'4" and weighing a whopping 150 soaking wet, he had the heart of a giant and his basketball skills reflected that.

By the beginning of the fourth quarter they approached a forty point lead, so Coach Woodward cleared his bench and gave the starters a rest. Before making that decision, Coach had already pulled Chris from the game minutes before the third quarter ended. The screams from the ecstatic crowd pressured Chris into putting on an array of fancy dribbling moves against his defender. With the entire building excitedly on their feet cheering, instead of Chris taking it in for an easy layup or passing off to a teammate for an assist, he brought the ball back to the top of the key and performed another series of crossover moves causing the defender to stumble to the ground. Chris then took a step back, way beyond the three point line, looked down at the defender and put up a high arching shot, hitting nothing but the bottom of the net! The game was temporarily delayed due to the amount of teenagers that swamped the court in reaction to the sensational moves Chris had just shown. Coach Woodward, acting as a traditional coach would, immediately substituted Chris out of the game for show boating. Once Chris left the game, the crowd showed extreme displeasure and stopped paying attention. While everyone mingled and contemplated on their next move, so were Chris and a few of his teammates.

"Man, y'all saw all those girls out there waving and choosin' a playa'." Chris teased in a feel good manner to a couple of his close buddies.

"Hell yeah!" His friend Randy replied. "Check it out tho', I got some'nt lined up for us tonight; didn't you say ya' moms 'nem was gone outta' town?"

"And you kno' 'dis!" Chris said, giving his best Chris Tucker impersonation.

"Good, cause I got some bad ass hoes that wanna get up wit us tonight."

"I'on kno' man, I see some right now that a nigga might try to get up wit'."

"Trust me dawg, these hoe's I'm talkin' 'bout is some fa'sho' pussy and they thick as hell!" Randy continued on with his persuading, "You know my sister go to that all girl high school, right? Well, the other day she brought her friend to the crib and soon as she saw a'pimp she chose..." Randy expressed himself in a 'Mack daddy' fashion as Chris and Dante jokingly let out long sighs of disbelief, accusing Randy of his usual exaggerating. "...Anyway, once I told her you was my home boy and invited her to the game, she pulled out her cell phone and showed me some pictures of her girls and them hoes was jus' as bad!"

"What makes you so sure they givin' up tha' ass?" Chris asked, cutting Randy's convincing speech short.

"Cumm'on dawg." Randy stared at him in utter disbelief before saying, "They be around nuttin' but pussy all day long, you kno' 'dey some freaks!"

"Where they at?" Dante attentively asked.

Once turning in the direction where the three young ladies and Randy's sister stood, they all looked at each other and were astounded! All three young women had a cute and seductive, but innocent college prep appearance. Not to mention his sister wasn't short stopping. Every one of them deserved to be on a version of America's Next Top Model! With thighs and ass bulging out of their skin tight jeans, the demeanor they had about themselves let off the energy of young gold diggers. It was no doubt in Chris and his friend's mind what their plans were after witnessing the young stallions posted up awaiting their arrival.

The game finally came to an end and the guys were anxious to hit the showers and be on their way. Paying little attention to the scolding Coach gave out for show boating, Chris and his buddies headed straight for the exit. While the rest of the team either took public transportation or waited on a sibling for a ride, Chris and his two comrades were in races to get to his souped-up Regal.

On the way to the car, the three of them passed by plenty of altercations. There were a couple of gang fights in progress, girls included. The police had a few streets blocked off in hopes of trying to stop the huge, angry crowds from fighting. Before making it to the car, a Shorty jets pass Chris hollering out, "Aey Lord, y'all hurry up and get the fuck up outta' here! It's fenna' go down!" That was their cue to speed up the process and get the hell out of dodge.

The girls had their own ride so they followed Chris to a much safer zone. After meeting each other and getting better acquainted, they all made further plans and agreed on being together for a night full of pleasure.

Chapter 11

On a trip to his home in the far south suburbs, Marcus was accompanied by a female that he begun to draw special interest in, Denise Hopkins A.K.A Niecey. Niecey was the first female to accompany Marcus to his family home. Niecey was different than most females Marcus dealt with. Her sex appeal was on the same level as Marcus's other women, but her family background was what distinguished her from the others. She grew up not wanting for anything. Her father was the head of his own law firm and her mother was the vice president over operations at a big time syndicate radio station in Chicago. Niecey and her parents lived in an extravagant home not too far from Marcus. Marcus actually met her at a Walgreens in the area and from that point on a strong chemistry had developed between the two.

Niecey worked with her mother as a program director. She earned her own money despite her parents being well off financially. Niecey's independence is what attracted Marcus the most; not to mention her humbleness, great sense of humor, and last but certainly not least, her beauty. Niecey stood about 5 foot 5 with heels. She had a butter pecan complexion and a sensual smile with deep dimples engraving her puffed cheeks. Niecey kept her full, shapely lips shiny with the finest lip gloss. Her bronze colored hair was cut in a short style with enough hair to cover her left eye. Most people would say she resembles the actress Elise Neal. Above all, Niecey's class level and swagger was well on a celebrity status which made her and Marcus a good look.

Pulling up to the house in his new model silver Corvette bumping the sounds of the Isley Brothers "Between the Sheets", Marcus reached up to his sun visor and pressed the garage door opener. He noticed an unfamiliar car parked alongside Chris' Regal in their drive way. By the model of the car Marcus took it as Chris having female company so he thought nothing of it, in fact, he was delighted to see his younger brother on some real player shit.

, Marcus had the key halfway in the door of the garage door entrance when the sounds of R. Kelly slow grooves caught them both off guard. After giving each other wide-eyed looks, they reluctantly stepped inside. Marcus noticed the music being played on the surround sound system that played through speakers in every room throughout the house. Before turning on any lights Marcus sensed different movements coming from the sectional sofa in the front room area. From the sounds of the music and by it being pitch black, it was obvious a real live sex scene was in progress. Marcus flicked on the lights and what was before his eyes infuriated him. A big orgy was taking place in the front room, where the family spends most of their time, and to make matters worse Chris wasn't involved in the action.

Marcus watched naked bodies nervously scattering around trying to cover themselves and in a low, short-tempered tone asked, "Where da fuck Chris at?"

"He, he, upstairs big bra," Randy stuttered out while hobbling on one leg as he struggled to put his pants on.

Marcus kicked off his shoes before creeping on the white mink carpet that lay in the very expensive and secluded living room area. The music drowned any other noise that went on in the house so it was impossible for Chris to hear any one come up the stairs. As Marcus got closer to his bedroom door he noticed it was slightly cracked. Marcus controlled his emotions and peeped in before busting through.

"Chriisssss, you like it..." the young, beautiful stallion murmured out in pure ecstasy while straddled on top of Chris in a cowgirl position, slowly grinding her hips to the rhythm of the beat.

"Hell yea...!" Chris passionately hummed out, obviously being caught in the moment. His hands gripped tight on her perfectly shaped apple bottom as she rode his dick from the back like a seasoned vet.

In between moaning and groaning she continuously cried out, "...It's y-o-u-r-s, take it, take it..."

Marcus found himself lost in the moment while admiring his little brother's choice of women. After a good minute or two of being awestruck, Marcus gathered himself and lightly tapped on the door. After his knocks were ignored he began to knock excessively. Breaking their chemistry, Chris reluctantly removed her from his lap and marched his naked body towards the door with a slight attitude. After seeing Marcus's face he stepped out the room, closing the door behind him.

"I need to holla' at'chu." Marcus's tone of voice and mean mug spoke volumes. Chris trailed his brother to the guest room with both hands cuffing his private area.

"Big bra, let me explain-" Chris began to say before getting cut off.

"Man, I'on wanna hear 'dat shit..." Marcus snapped while managing to sustain a mild mannered tone. "...You got these niggas at our crib fuckin' on the couch momma lay her head on...fuck is wrong wit'chu'!"

"I told them go upstairs to the guest room."

"That ain't the point, why -n- the fuck you got them out here, anyway? You kno' damn well I'on need nobody in the 'hood knowin' where we lay our head at!"

"They ain't on shit like--"

"You don't know that," Marcus cut him off. "They be in the 'hood jus' like everybody else...!"

Marcus sensed an attitude coming from Chris. With fury in his eyes, Marcus went on to say, "…Look, I'on mind you having certain females out here, that's cool; but if you ever, I mean ever, bring some niggas out here again, we gon' have a big problem. Now you got 'til the morning to get them mothafuckas out my crib!"

"I got'chu big bra'. It won't happen again, that's my word." Chris sincerely apologized after seeing Marcus meant business. Chris definitely didn't want to see his brother's ugly side so he immediately took control of the situation. Marcus didn't spoil the night entirely, he allowed them to resume their rendezvous, but in a more respectable manner. He was actually digging how his little brother was handling his business in the bedroom.

As Chris got his company squared away Marcus made his way back to his date. Walking up to a giggly Denise, Marcus asked, "What'chu laughin' at? Ain't nuttin funny." He stated half-heartedly.

"Did you see how they were scrambling around looking for they stuff?! Ass and titties was flying everywhere!" She teased in the midst of laughter. "They were in here getting they freak on!"

I couldn't help but see all 'dat ass… Marcus simply shook his head as he recollected to himself. Marcus admired their style of women, but disliked how Chris went about it due to safety purposes.

Marcus and his companion departed down to the basement where they ended their night out with sparks. The fully furnished basement was like a mini condo within the mansion. It was decked out. It became Marcus's man cave.

Chapter 12

Marcus had made several attempts to pay for all of Lil Reesie's funeral arrangements but his grandmother, his primary guardian, rejected all of his offers due to her beliefs. After realizing that her only option was to let the state bury her grandson, she broke down and accepted the help.

The funeral service took place on a Saturday morning. Marcus sponsored the funeral, but Reesie's grandmother insisted on having a respectable service at her long time, small, hole in the wall Baptist church. The church was located on the corner of the same block where Reesie was murdered. It was so close to the site, all people had to do was step outside and look down the block to see the memorial that the neighborhood put together for him: Everything from teddy bears, liquor bottles, and large posters with pictures and everyone's comments and condolences.

The small church was packed as most people stood in a long line to view the body. Every step a person took made the uneven, carpeted floor squeak. The ceiling even had a few leaks. Nonetheless, everyone from the 'hood still went to pay their respects. The majority of the people who came to the funeral wore special made t-shirts with Reesie's face and the dates of his birth and death.

The enormously sad funeral was dramatic. All the kids from off 21st were deeply hurt to see one of their own inside a casket. You even had a few females passing out from being so emotional. The 'hood knew what type of lifestyle Reesie led but they weren't ready to grasp the situation. With a custom made black and gold casket with a suit to match, Marcus had Reesie going out in style.

When Marcus arrived to the funeral, he was immediately escorted by his security straight to the casket without waiting in the long line. Marcus pecked Reesie's stiff cheek and said a prayer over the casket before consoling the family that sat in the front row. When he embraced the grandmother she uncontrollably broke down in his arms. Once everyone noticed Marcus being there, all the attention began turning his way. Marcus hated attending funerals so he left before the service was over.

Standing outside of the church to escape all of the drama, Marcus stood in the middle of all the Lords that attended the service. In their brief meeting, everyone was insinuating on who they thought could've pulled off such a clever murder. A few names popped up, but the one name that stuck out more than others was none other than Nutso. Nutso was missing in action before and after the incident, which wasn't unusual. When it was all said and done everyone suspected it to be an unauthorized hit within the mob.

Being a five star elite of any branch within the Nation carried a heavy load and for Rico it was no different. Though Rico was rich and getting paper, he and Marcus approached the streets in different manners. Rico was more power struck. He wanted his name ringing around the city as that nigga who lay down all the laws and ran majority of the street operations for the IVL's under Chief Marcus. Unlike the last five star that sat in the seat before him, Rico was more loyal to the Nation and he honored Marcus for his street knowledge and cleverness. Marcus let Rico roam freely and do whatever he felt, as long as it was brought to his attention first. Marcus preferred to live his life on more of a low key note these days, but at times that was impossible due to his citywide status. Marcus was definitely a feared killer in the streets. In contrast to Rico's boldness, when a personal hit was a must, Marcus moved like a thief in the night. Rico sent out hits with his stamp. He wanted niggas to not only feel his pain, but also know who issued it. Rico's surge for dominance often started unnecessary wars and Marcus had to either squash the drama or back it.

"I wonder what Erica been up to..." Marcus muttered to himself while joyriding through downtown in his 'Vette. He began scrolling through the contact list on his phone and started reviewing his options of women to call. "...Damn, I ain't heard from Tasha in'a while, she prob'le still mad at me. Maybe I'a get up wit' Nicole sexy ass for'a lunch date... naaahhh. Niecey, that's who I need to see." Marcus was zoning out from the blunt he was smoking to the face which usually made him contemplate thoughts out loud when alone.

As he sent the call through to Niecey, it was interrupted by an unfamiliar number. Instead of ignoring the unknown caller like he normally does, curiosity took effect.

"Hello!" Marcus answered in a defensive tone.

"Lord, you around somewhere? I need to bump into you." Marcus caught on to Rico's voice immediately. In that instant, Marcus mindset went from pleasure to street business.

"I'll be around in'a minute. Why? Wassup?"

"You know I'ont like talkin' over these horns like that. How long it's gon' take you to get out west?"

"Gimme 'bout 20 minutes."

"You wanna meet towards the headquarters?" Rico asked. The headquarters was considered the Holy City, 16th Street.

"Naw, I'll come wherever you at."

"A'ight. Call me when you in route."

Marcus wasn't strapped at the time of the call because he was running errands downtown, but once he got the call to report to the trenches, he made a quick stop to pick up the stainless steel. It wasn't that he didn't trust Rico or felt endangered; this was just his street instinct. Marcus knew he would be meeting Rico in a high crime neighborhood that the Vice Lords governed so solid security was certain; especially when one of the Chiefs came anywhere around the premises.

Pulling up on Chicago Avenue and Pulaski was no different than pulling up anywhere in the Holy City. Marcus was recognizable everywhere as a Chief and his status was known city wide. People clinged to him like white on rice. Before Rico arrived on the scene, Marcus had gathered a nice crowd around him. This land was where Rico was made and one of the main areas he had a tight hold on.

Rico hopped out of his wood grain painted Jeep Cherokee with a sense of urgency. He was pleased to see Marcus comfortable amongst his personal comrades. Rico not only demanded respect for himself within the mob, but he always enforced Marcus's name as being a stand up leader. So whenever Marcus popped up in any of their territories he never encountered any unexpected acts of betrayal.

All attention turned toward Rico as he walked up to the four man crowd. After shaking up with everybody and getting the inside scoop on the block, Rico directed his conversation toward Marcus while the others stood and listened.

"I been taking care of Nation bin'nis out there in them Wild Hunits," Rico began, referring to the far South side of Chicago. "The joint out there been doin' numbers since we opened up. I been working with the Lords from out there and I found out they ain't as strong as I need them to be. I went out there and laid the law down, now you got all type of niggas comin' out the blue tryna' claim some shit."

Marcus stood there and listened while observing how the block they were posted up on was being operated.

"What make it so bad, these niggas ain't even on law and claim they got blessed in by some ole school cats that nobody honor or know."

"What names they hollerin' out there?" Marcus asked.

"Invalid names that I can't even remember. See, back in the day a few straggling Lords migrated out there and started their own mob of Insanes. They was deep at one point and took over a 'hood that belonged to the other side. The niggas who started the movement got killed not too long after and they been fucked up out there ever since."

"You went out there and put 'dem niggas on. So what's the problem?" Marcus asked with concern, obviously trying to get to the root of the situation.

"The niggas that 'posed to be runnin' shit out there, I left them out the operation and used the shorties. Now that they see shit starting to pick up, they wanna' try to make some noise." The few that stood amongst them felt honored and empowered to be around two high profiled figures as they conversed. Rico went on to say, "They sent a so called message and murked two of the Lords from out there that I had runnin' 'da block. I was really thinkin' 'bout goin' on'a fuckin' rampage and kill 'dem niggas and anybody close to 'em; I mean an all-out warfare jus' to let them chumps know who they fuckin' wit!" Rico expressed himself hot tempered.

"We cain't get money and go to war at the same time," Marcus reassured. "Now do you think the land out there is worth going to war over?"

"If it what'nt Chief, I wouldn't of even brought it to your attention."

"Okay then, I suggest you close down shop and knock the two heads off and I guarantee you everything else will fall into place. Sometimes it doesn't take killin' up an entire 'hood to get'cho' point across."

Rico stood there and listened like class was in session. Rico had been in the game just as long as Marcus, but he knew Marcus had taken several important hits for the mob in the past. He valued his knowledge when it came to the rules of engagement.

After discussing the situation with Marcus, Rico contemplated on a solution to the problem. More than likely he was going to take Marcus's advice by doing his homework and strapping up with a couple of the mob'sknown silencers to take care of the business. Rico had no problem shutting down the spot out south due to the fact that all the other areas he had control over throughout the West Side were making major dollars. Out south was a new project he took upon himself to make prosperous.

Marcus was confident that Rico would take care of the problem he provoked. If need be, Marcus knew what to do if the situation caused more time and bloodshed than necessary. Being that Marcus was the go-to man for both, the Conservatives and the Insanes, he had access to more than his share of professional hit men. Not to mention the qualities of being one himself.

These were the type of problems that accosted Marcus on a day to day basis. Whether they were big or small he dealt with them accordingly. Marcus was fortunate to have grown up around major mob figures like Big C because it groomed his state of mind. His precise decision making was turning him into a seasoned Chief.

Chapter 13

"Let me get'a half gallon of gin and a box of blunts."

"What kind?" The Arabic liquor store owner asked with a thick accent.

"I come to 'dis ma'fuckin' sto' every day and you still don't know what kind'a blunts I need?!" the young, wannabe gangster yelled out. "...Gimme a box of White Owls; and let that be the last time I have to remind ya ass, a'ight!"

"You fucking threaten me?!"

"Fuck you, Ali! You lucky you behind that thick ass glass or else I'a beat that ass!"

"Fuck you! Keep talking that shit, I'll ban your ass from my store for good this time!" He responded while fulfilling the order. The Arabic store owner had become accustomed to the everyday harassment that he endured from the young hoodlums and most of the customers from the neighborhood.

The young thug and two of his fellow bangers were getting prepared to indulge in their nightly ritual. They knew no other way to vent after a long day of putting in work on the blocks. Drinking, smoking, and fucking different females was their definition of enjoying the 'fruits of your labor'.

One of the youngsters stated to the other two, "Man, if these hoes ain't talkin' 'bout nothin', we gon' spin off before they drink up all our shit."

"I'm wit' 'dat. They ain't nuttin' but some buss downs anyway. They should already kno' what time it is!" They all gave each other dap while waiting on their goods.

The driver of an old, rusted out Grand Marquis with temp plates and heavily tinted windows, barked out as he passed by the liquor store on the corner of 19th and Kedzie, "Listen man, when I bend back around, y'all bail out and let 'dem bitch ass niggas have it soons they step out the sto'!" He was accompanied by three other Lords, they took it upon themselves to ride down on the opposition. The shorties off 21st still had a sour taste in their mouth about the unsolved murder of their fellow Lord, Lil Reesie. They were impatient and became agitated for not having anyone in particular to retaliate against so they decided to pay their rival gang a special visit.

After turning the corner of 19th they slowly pulled on the side of the store and turned off the headlights.

"Aey, y'all make this shit quick," the driver spoke in a low pitched tone. "...Knock 'dem niggas off and let's get the fuck outta' here!"

Everyone's adrenaline was on high as they locked and loaded their artillery.

"Hell yea, 'dis for you Reesie!" one of the Lords blurted out in a crazed manner as he angrily cocked back the stainless steel.

"Gaddamn Ali! It took yo' ass long enough'! Matt-a-fact, get me a pack of Newports why you at it!" the young thug hollered out.

"You need to make up your mind muthafucker!" Ali retorted in his heavy accent, only to have the youngsters burst into laughter. They always got a kick out of getting the foreigner aggravated. They loved to hear him curse back.

After leaving the liquor store with the proper goods to set their night off, nothing more was on their mind other than partying the night out. The last thing they were expecting was an attack against them on familiar grounds.

"Aey G, don't get this liquor in ya' system and start drivin' all crazy-n-shit," one of the shorties stated half-heartedly.

"What? Nigga, you scared? You need to be worried about if these hoes you putting us on givin' up 'dat ass tonight, 'cause if not, I'ma make yo' ass walk back!" Shorty jokingly threatened as they strolled toward a gray Pontiac Bonneville.

Two of the Lords, dressed in regular clothing and black ski masks, crept along the blind side of the liquor store with their pistols drawn, ready to deliver. After a few more steps toward the car, one of the shorties instinctively glanced behind him. In that instant his life flashed right before his!

"OH SHIT!!!" He hysterically screamed out in a desperate attempt to break away. The other two followed suit with no questions asked. A split second later rapid shots polluted the night air sounding like a thunderous storm.

The two gunmen were recklessly letting off shots, not caring who was in sight or what they hit. If it wasn't so late in the morning, innocent bystanders would've easily been involved in the crossfire. After emptying the clips to both semi-automatics, the Lords wildly ran back to the car. Although the job was sloppily done, all three targets were fatally shot and the Bonneville was filled with holes. The unorganized adolescents fled the scene feeling good, not knowing if they killed something or not.

While Marcus sponsored a war out South concerning Rico, another one was developing right under his nose.

Chapter

14

Marcus and J.R. sat at the kitchen table at an occupied residence that Marcus had all access to. Here is where he packaged and separated all the work that was to be issued out amongst the mob. The two-level home was stationed on a low key block right outside the 'hood. The residents were a family that Marcus grew up knowing. Ever since he adopted them as family, they went from poverty to living 'ghetto fabulous'.

When it came time to take care of business, Marcus never parked any of his noticeable cars around the area or he either drove with someone else. This particular residence was also where he redirected all important jail calls, specifically calls that came from Smitty, who was doing his bid in the Feds. Marcus wasn't around to receive majority of the calls; he would only get shortened messages. Marcus made sure Smitty was financially comfortable during his stay in the Feds, but as time progressed Marcus gave little thought to their constant miscommunication. As far as Marcus was concerned, he was now the reigning Chief over the IVL's and Smitty was history for the moment.

"How we been goin' through this shit, I kno' Kunta gotta be a happy man," J.R. spoke while making the proper measurements for each package. J.R. was the only person in the crew that actually saw Kunta in person. The others merely speculated or just went off of what Marcus told them. "You think he supplying anybody else in the city wit' this good shit?"

"Man, dude showed me a whole 'nother side to him," Marcus replied as he smoked and watched J.R. work the Pyrex.

"This mothafucka got businesses out the ass. He jus' recently showed me around a carpet warehouse that he owns."

"Straight up," J.R. reacted surprisingly while keep his eyes on the task at hand.

"That ain't the half of it," Marcus began to explain. "The nigga took me to his personal area in the back and showed me two walls stacked to the ceiling wit' bricks and keys of dope. He claimed everything there was for me, but'chu never kno' wit' these foreigners; they can get real slick."

They continued on with the small talk while taking of care business. Out of nowhere a familiar voice in the house hollered out, "Marcus, is that you up there?"

"Yeah, it's me Granma Betty; you ain't got to worry ya'self."

"Awe baby, I what'nt worried," she loudly shot back. "'Cause if it was anybody else other than you, baby, I was coming up shooting!" She finished her statement with a laugh. Marcus and J.R laughed at her bold statement they knew she was dead serious.

"Son, make sure you come holla' at me before you leave, ya' hear."

"I got'chu' Momma."

Betty was the grandmother of the household. She was one of those elders that acted 20 years younger than her actual age. She knew all about the game. Some even labeled her as the queen of the Holy City from past relationships that she had with a few known neighborhood drug lords from back in the day.

Marcus loved her like a mother. Those close to him knew he took her in as his 'play momma'. All Momma Betty's biological children were grown and either strung out on dope or locked up. Betty was a gansta'. She always spoke her mind and never sugarcoated anything. Unlike Sylvia and Grandma Emma, Marcus was able to talk to Momma Betty about street activities. She would give him valuable advice on how to play street guys and plenty of game on gold digging females, so it was safe to say Marcus peeped game from a mile away.

A couple hours of putting in work at the table was ending as they labeled the designated packages. It was J.R. and Peewee's job to deliver the packages to certain individuals that controlled different blocks around the city. Rico and Kunta were the only two people Marcus made hand to hand transactions with.

Deciding not to wait on Marcus to come see her, Betty took it upon herself to march from the basement up to the first floor. With a cordless house phone glued to her ear, Betty came through the first floor doors and headed directly towards the kitchen. She had no problem seeing all kinds of drug paraphernalia in her kitchen; back in the day she was around that type of environment on a daily basis.

"Good, I thought you snuck up outta' here without telling me like you always do." Betty claimed while handing over the phone to Marcus. The scrunched expression Marcus displayed made it obvious that he disapproved of the phone call at that time. He wasn't interested in conversing with anyone outside of his immediate surroundings.

"Chile' don't be looking all ugly in the face," Betty said after feeling the uneasiness come from Marcus. "You better take this call."

"Who is this?" Marcus silently asked with one hand covering the receiver.

"If you put'cha' ear to the phone, you'll see." Marcus put the phone to his ear and calmly spoke, "Yeah, who 'dis?"

The caller chuckled and said, "What's going on young fella'? How is life treating you out there in the free world?"

After catching on to the distinctive voice on the other end, Marcus's facial expression remained the same.

"I can't call it," he replied in a somewhat irritable tone.

"Long time no hear...I take it life must be treating you pretty well out there."

"Due to the circumstances, I can't complain," Marcus replied. The conversation with Smitty was stale. Because their communication was basically nonexistent, the discomfort level was easily sensed. To make matters worse, Marcus disliked the fact that he was talking on a land line with a high profile kingpin. The last thing he needed was his voice to be recorded by federal agents.

"It's been damn near a whole year since I last heard from you. If it what'nt for my other connections to the streets, I wouldn't know what was going on wit'chu," Smitty stated sounding more concerned than angry.

"You know how I am about these phones; I stay away from 'em," Marcus hinted.

"It's other ways to stay in tune. I fly kites out all the time and still get no response," Smitty retorted. "But anyway, it's some serious shit goin' on around you that I need to inform you on. If it ain't dealt wit' accordingly, it could fuck up everything." Marcus kept complete silence while closely listening to his leader.

"Hello!" Smitty hollered out as if the call was lost.

"Yeah, yeah I'm here," Marcus muttered.

"I mean, you know I don't like to conduct business this way either. I'ma send a kite out this week, so keep a heads up.

"I copy that."

"I kno' I been missing in action for'a minute, but I ain't got long before I touchdown. I'm already on my fifth term."

Since Marcus took the active role as Chief of the IVL Nation in '95, his power in the streets was growing rapidly. These days, the up and coming generation was only honoring Marcus as their respected street leader. Smitty's name was slowly leaving their memory banks. With so much going on around him, Marcus never took the time to realize how close it was to Smitty's return.

"Yeah, time has been flyin'," Marcus began to say. "But you don't need to worry. Ery'thing in good hands out here. That's my word."

"That's what I need to hear," Smitty said, sounding like a load had been lifted off his shoulders.

"Oh yea, I been getting that weekly package, too. I been straight on that end; it's jus' the communication part needs to get a lot better."

After a few more words the call was ended. As if Marcus didn't have enough problems on his plate, he now had to contemplate on whatever situation Smitty was referring to. Marcus had begun to wonder how Smitty would come home and approach the streets. Would he come home on a power trip?

Or would he be willing to step back and let Marcus continue his reign as the active Chief of the IVL's?

Marcus snapped out of his deep trance and set up all of J.R. and Peewee's drop offs before going on about his day. Although his money was tapping into the seven figures, his problems were accumulating just as fast.

15

Sitting on the sectional in the front room at the crib out South, Steve and Big C sat back and touched base on different subjects while enjoying a Sunday afternoon Bears game. Although the house Marcus purchased was extravagant, Big C's homes weren't short stopping, heowned more than one mansion.

As they drank on their Crown Royal Reserve, their conversation concerning the street game suddenly took an awkward turn.

"We groomed us one, didn't we." Big C stated while setting his drinking glass on top of a nearby coaster.

"We groomed us one?" Steve questioned, not really having a clue where Big C was headed with his statement.

"I'm sayin', look around you. That boy done came up!" He expressed excitedly while taking a glance around the house as if it was his first visit.

"Awe, hell yeah, he handles his business." Steve agreed after realizing Big C was referring to Marcus.

"I mean, for the brotha' to be making so much money at such a young age, he carries himself wit' much integrity and respect. Every young nigga that came before him that got blessed wit' some juice, they either misused their power and got dealt wit' or caught major cases.

"Yeah, he's definitely one of a kind," Steve agreed. "It ain't often that a young Chief come along and stay down on law and move around so swiftly."

Before replying, Big C stared off into space as if he was pondering on what to say next. After sipping his drink he blurted out, "I was a little worried at first, I thought after he climbed the ladder of success, them bad traits of his ole man was gon' come out of him. You kno', on that renegade shit. I would've hated to do him like we had to that nigga." Big C stated in his normal horrific tone.

Big C's sudden statement caught Steve by complete surprise. He knew Marcus's father was a victim to some slimy street shit, but never knew Big C was the actual gunman. Over the years there were many speculations on his murder. Big C always claimed the situation was out of his hands and knew nothing about the setup. At this very moment Steve was feeling a sense of dishonesty and betrayal.

Not really wanting to question his leader, Steve loosely asked, "What, you put a price on his head or some shit?"

"Don't tell me you done forgot?" Big C said as if he was taking Steve back down memory lane. "That nigga was becoming a real threat. He didn't wanna convert over to the Nation. He was beginning to think he was untouchable. Hell, if you ask me, he was prob'le ready to whack yo' ass for taking his woman." Big C talked liked he was legitimizing his wrongdoings.

"All these years I never knew it was an inside job, tho'."

"You should've known that," Big C shot back. "Look man, that nigga was a loose cannon. Robbing the brothers in the neighborhood, I mean, it had to be done! That mothafucka had ery'body in the 'hood shook up from the head count he had under his belt so I had to strap up and take care of 'dat bin'nis myself. I never told you because I didn't need you making no excuses for that chump!" As Big C talked, it seemed as if enmity was still built up inside.

Steve sat there puzzled, but his facial expression showed otherwise. He couldn't wear his emotions on his sleeve, especially around such a huge street figure like Big C.

All this damn time I couldn't tell this boy who killed his pops and the man himself been up under our nose. Steve remorsefully thought to himself as they zoomed back in on the Bears game.

Steve's train of thought was soon interrupted by the sound of the alarm system signaling that someone had entered the home. Steve was expecting

Sylvia to come through the doors at any time of the day.

"Babes, I got C in here wit' me," he spoke out, giving his wife a heads up about company being over.

"Damn ole man, I know you got love for me, but I can't be yo' baby." Marcus snickered while shaking his head as he made his way through the garage door entrance.

Marcus caught Steve and Big C both by surprise and this led to few seconds of awkward silence. Marcus very rarely made an appearance to the house this early in the day and it didn't help they were previously discussing a critical topic that had plagued Marcus's mental over the years.

"I what'nt expecting to see you. What's goin' on?" Steve said, breaking the temporary silence as he stood to his feet.

"This the only time I seem to get some real rest." In the same breath Marcus walked over to properly greet Big C. "Chief, what brings you outta' the house this early in the day?" They embraced each other with a formal hug as they met face to face.

"Ya' daddy got me over here watchin' these sorry ass Bears," Big C responded in an amused tone. Marcus never came to the point of calling Steve his daddy, but he wasn't going to correct the long lived Chief. "I see you still doin' the right thane."

"I'on kno' no other way to be, Chief. I learned from the best." Marcus said, looking Big C square in the eye then glancing back at Steve, giving them both proper acknowledgements.

Looking as though he was touched by Marcus statement Big C said, "I swear I couldn't think of nobody else better to take care of my mob."

Marcus was the active leader over the IVL's, but he supplied all the leaders of the CVL mob through Big C. The Conservatives always respected Big C as the King of their Nation, but they were beginning to honor Marcus as their breadwinner. Marcus had a unique position with VL's on the West Side of Chicago and his clout was growing by the day.

As long as Marcus kept the six figure check coming in every month, Big C had no issues with him.

"I know this shit can get real hectic out here, especially with you having so much on ya' plate," Big C sincerely expressed himself. "You kno' if the load get too heavy I'm--" Marcus cut him short of his statement.

"With all due respect, Chief, I got this." He respectfully reassured, "Y'all jus' sit back and chill. Believe me, you'll kno' when I need you.

Big C let out a busted laugh before saying, "See, that's what I'm talkin' 'bout!" He exclaimed in between laughs. He inched closer to Marcus and placed both hands on his cheeks and said with a devious smirk, "Chief Marcus!"

Steve was standing in the background observing the façade. He and Big C caught eyes and that's when Steve noticed the all too familiar terror forming in the eyes of Big C.

All these years you had resentment towards me, now here it is you huggin' the man who was behind the trigga'. Steve shamefully thought to himself as he looked on.

"Come on, sit down here and have a drink wit' us," Big C insisted.

"I wish I could, but I'm tired as hell." Marcus yawned showing his exhaustion. "I'm finna' go up here and pass out."

Watching Marcus make his way towards the stairs, Big C chanted, "ALMIGHTY!" Marcus proudly chanted back without breaking stride towards the stairs.

During the remainder of Big C's stay, there was little conversation between the two as they resumed watching the Bears game. Big C had no clue of how passionate Marcus felt about his father being murdered in cold blood. Big C figured since Marcus was such a young kid when it happened that it was a dead issue.

Steve was contemplating breaking the news to Marcus. He had built up a significant amount of gratitude for Marcus over the years of his reign at the top. Steve knew if the shocking news was revealed to Marcus it could possibly result in the assassination of Big C, which would mean a war within the Nation. That's the one thing Steve wanted to avoid.

16

The over packed gym was in pandemonium as they all got set for the championship game of an annual Christmas tournament featuring the Westinghouse Warriors and the Crane Admirals. Both were undefeated and well respected for their basketball programs. Steve was amongst the cheering crowd. Fans were there to watch both teams, but most of the people were there to witness the number one ranked point guard in the country, Chris. Chris was only a junior and being scouted by the top Division I colleges in the country.

While the entire crowd's minds were on the game, Chris's mind was focused on the different females in the bleachers. During warm-ups Chris was seen waving at different females that he had sexual encounters with in the past.

"Look at 'Iesha 'nem over there." Chris spoke to a teammate in the layup line.

"Yeah, I see her, but who is ole girl sittin' next to her?" His teammate sensuously asked while pointing.

"I don't kno' who she is, but I do kno' she fine as hell, tho'."

Once the tip went in the air, Chris got right down to business hitting his first five shots giving the Bulldogs an early lead. After every shot he made Chris threw up the VL sign at the crowd. "CHRIS!!! Keep 'ya head in the damn game!" Steve stood to his feet and hollered out. Steve's intensity level always stayed on high when attending important games.

Although the Admirals had good players that played well together, they lacked an all-American. They were still able to go undefeated early on in the season. Despite having good players, the team had no answer for Chris, who seemed to be putting on a show for the energized crowd.

"CLEAR OUT! CLEAR OUT!" Chris yelled out as he waived off a set play. He dribbled between his legs four times before performing a cross over move that had his defender off balance. With a clear path to the hole Chris threw up a sensational alley-oop to his center that brought the house down!

While most of the crowd was reacting to the tremendous play, right beside Steve commotion amongst a group of female fans was forming.

"Gurrrl, you see my boo out there killin' 'ney ass!" A young female loudly boasted on Chris's performance to her friends next to her, not knowing there was a 'hood girl a row back who claimed to be Chris's main lady.

"I know 'dis bitch jus' didn't call my man, her boo?" The young, shameless diva stated amongst her group.

"Yes she did gurl!" Her friend replied, edging the situation on.

"Uh uh, I'm fenna' check this hoe," she said while making her way down the bleachers with three rough looking girls following behind. She calmly tapped on the young lady shoulder before boldly asking, "Excuse me, ummm, did I jus' hear you call my man, boo?"

The young lady gave off a disgusted expression before saying, "I'm sorry, I don't know who yo' man 'posed to be, but I was talkin' 'bout Chris, sweetie." "Uh-uh, no she didn't..." The girls who trailed behind instigated.

Both females were cute and had nice bodies. But it was obvious they were on two different class levels. One was a 'hood chick and the other was a suburban girl.

Steve's focus left the game after overhearing Chris name being mentioned. It forced him to tune into the drama.

"Bitch, you must be confused. Not only am I pregnant wit' Chris' baby, but everybody and 'ney momma knows I'm wifey!" The young reckless female blurted out an obvious lie, drawing more attention to the nonsense.

The classier of the two seemed to be backing down from the altercation. She countered intelligently with, "Look...I'm here to enjoy a basketball game. Your issue seems to be wit' Christopher."

"Naw bitch! I got my issue wit' the right one!"

"You need to watch who the fuck you callin' a b---"

SMACK! In midsentence, the young aggressor connected with a wild, open handed right that landed flush on the other girl's cheek. Surprisingly the other girl had a cat-like reflex and immediately retaliated by landing a punch of her own. In an instant an all-out scuffle between both parties was in progress. With hands swinging and bodies falling, a few civilized adults muscled through the crowd to settle the mini brawl down before it got too out of hand. Due to the excitement of the game, no one outside of that particular section was paying attention to the commotion.

Steve didn't bother to get involved with the conflict. He was stuck standing still with only two words rambling through his brain, "Pregnant? Wifey? I need to holla' at this lil' dude." Steve mumbled to himself as he watched the two female groups get separated.

By halftime the Bulldogs were up by ten points. Chris was putting on a show in the first half, scoring 25 of the Bulldogs 40 points. Once the team began jogging toward the tunnel, on their way to the locker room, Steve eagerly made his way towards their direction.

After getting past security, Steve made it to the locker room and found Coach Woodward in the middle of lecturing his team. Steve politely hand signaled the coach to allow him to talk with Chris.

With a towel in hand, wiping the beads of sweat from his forehead, Chris stepped out the door.

"What's goin' on Pops?" Chris was breathing heavily as he continued to wipe the sweat from his face.

"Aey keep doin' ya' thane." Steve started the conversation by complimenting his son and giving him a shoulder to shoulder dap.

"You saw how I broke dude ankles," Chris bragged excitedly as he reenacted the dribbling move he displayed earlier in the game. "These dudes can't guard me. I'm really finna' kill 'em in the second half."

"Yeah, yeah I see you out there, but wassup wit' this shit I see you throwing up after every basket. What, you gang banging now?" Steve questioned with pure fury.

"Awe, nah Pop, that's jus' somen't I do to get the crowd pumped up."

"Let that be the last time I see that shit, a'ight. You got major scouts in the crowd checkin' you out and the last thing you need is some bad press coming your way," Steve mildly chastised his son. Before stepping off, Steve blurted out, "And what's this shit I hear about you got some lil wild bitch pregnant?"

"Huh?" Chris was caught off guard by the question.

"Look, don't worry about it. We'll talk about that later. You jus go out there and keep ya' head in the game... and quit showboatin' so much!"

Chris stood there and listened to his father throughout most of the half-time break. Since he was the number one point guard in the state, Chris knew it was vital for him to play a more respectable game. So, he came out in the second half more focused on the game itself.

Even though Chris came out more efficient, the beginning of the third quarter belonged to the Crane Admirals as they put together a 10-2 run, slicing the Warriors lead down to two points. By his actions on the court in the second half, it was obvious that something had come over Chris and it was affecting the momentum of his team. Instead of him playing with the fierceness that the fans were accustomed to witnessing, he was busy instructing and playing like a traditional point guard. It cost the Bulldogs the lead and they were looking at a 68 to 60 deficit by the end of the third quarter.

While the crowd began showing extreme displeasure towards Westinghouse's second half performance, Coach Woodward scolded his team during the quarter break.

"How many times have we practiced this 2-3 zone defense?" Coach yelled in the huddle with his assistants standing beside him. He got no response. "You guys act like y'all don't know what the hell is goin' on out there! Randy, I tell you time and time again to cut off all penetration on the baseline; it shouldn't be any reason their point guard should be getting in the lane so easy!" During his speech, Coach seemed to be focusing on everybodys mistakes except Chris' until the buzzer sounded to report back to the court. "Chris! I need your focus back into the game...! On three, 1, 2, 3..."

"DEFENSE!!!" The team energetically roared.

Chris came out of the time out still playing conservatively, he allowed his fellow teammates to take charge, which worked out for the better. With Crane's defense focusing entirely on stopping Chris it gave the rest of the team the green light to step up their game. That led to a late fourth quarter rally that tied the game up at 80 apiece.

It came down to the last possession of the game and the Warriors were down two. Crane, still taking precaution, made it tough for the in bounder to get the ball to Chris and forced the Bulldogs to call their final 30 second timeout. During the timeout, Coach drew up a play that would open Chris up to receive the inbound pass.

After forcing a pass in to Chris, the Warriors barely made it across half without a violation as Chris dribbled his way through a ferocious full-court press. With 20 seconds left on the clock, Chris set up a motion offense at the top of the key. With the seconds ticking down, Chris attacked the basket only to run into a double team. Instead of creating a difficult move to attempt the tying basket, he conventionally dished the ball to an open teammate for a three point shot. Not being used to taking buzzer beaters, the player nervously took the shot. The ball swerved around, touching every part of the rim before coming out. The rebound was secured by the opposing team and the Warriors suffered their first loss of the season.

Chris had fascinating numbers. He scored 32 points, made 12 assist, pulled down 5 rebounds, got 6 steals, and even received the MVP honors, but he was still criticized by the press for not taking the last shot. Some even wondered if his sudden new style of play would prevent the Warriors from making it down state to compete for the title.

17

Posted up in one of his low key apartments in the congested but elaborate downtown area, Marcus stood silently dissecting a letter that was brought to him by J.R. and Peewee.

To whom it may concern:

The past five years I have been in this hell hole wondering how I got into this situation. I took good care of a lot of people out there and I always respected the streets and did things the right way. I always knew there were brothers amongst the Nation that had hatred built up in their hearts for whatever reason, but what family don't have that? What I'm about to tell you, young brotha', is going to shock you as it did me. The penitentiary where I'm at there are huge figures from different branches that passes through. It's one older brotha' in particular that revealed something to me that had me fucked up! All this time I could never put a finger on who these crackers were getting their leads from. And to think, if I only knew what I know now, I would have never joined forces with the enemy....In order to stop this disease from spreading and killing off our growing Nation we must find a cure before its too late. The only possible cure is to figure out where the problem starts and killing it off! I know it seems like an impossible mission but if it doesn't get done, you gone end up in this position next or somewhere worse. Believe me, I'm not the only one giving the green light. It's a few other heavyweights that he helped put behind these walls. Unfortunately some of those brothers will never see the light of day ever again! I have faith in you and I know you going to do the right thing. With that said, the next time I hear from you, this situation should be took care of and I expect the Nation to continue on striving for prosperity...I know things are tough out there in that wicked world but it won't be long before I'm back...

P.S. Tell your pops to open his eyes...The disease right beside him...

MIGHTY!"

Even though the letter lacked details and no names were mentioned Marcus was able to read between the lines. He understood exactly who Smitty was referring to. Smitty labeling Big C as a snitch shocked him to say the least. Not only was Big C one of the few originals still active amongst the Nation, but this was someone Marcus had looked up to throughout his childhood years and even as an adult.   Marcus   couldn't   imagine   himself assassinating someone of such magnitude, especially a man who he learned so much from.

While his two main guys played the video game as if they had no worries in the world, Marcus sat back periodically glancing at the letter in disbelief. He wondered if there was any truth in what he just read or if Smitty's personal feelings were getting in the way of his train of thought. Whatever the situation, Marcus knew the wrong reaction would be critical. He had to inform Steve in order to get a better understanding of what needed to be done.

Marcus didn't let the disturbing news distract him. After counting all the money that was collected by J.R. and Peewee from all the blocks in the Holy City, he squared them away with their generous, weekly paychecks. He didn't even bother telling them about the letter. All of Marcus's guys were IVL's and they had honored Smitty way before Marcus became Chief. They always acknowledged Big C as one of the originals and knew he was a very powerful and highly respected man, but if Smitty had ever declared war with the Conservatives, they would've jumped in a heartbeat. The only reason their respect level grew so much for Big C and his mob was because of the strong ties that he and Marcus built over the years. The last thing Marcus needed was an all-out war to break loose between the two mobs that he governed. He made up his mind to keep the news discreet until the situation unraveled.

Being caught up in everyday street activities often caused Marcus to neglect quality time with the family who loved him the most.

"Hello." Marcus answered his ringing Nextel in a modest tone after noticing a call coming in from the house out South.

"Heeeeey, this yo' momma," Sylvia announced on the other end in an entertaining tone as if her first born wouldn't recognize her voice.

"I know who this is, Ma," Marcus shot back. "What's goin' on?"

Sylvia burst out into laughter before stating, "I'on know now. I haven't heard from you in so long."

"I know Ma, I know. I gotta get better."

Sylvia had caught Marcus during his leisure time. Currently he was riding through the city on a pleasant afternoon with one of his lady friends, Shaunte. Although Niecey was demanding more of

Marcus attention these days he still had different females for different reasons.

Shaunte was the ride, smoke-n-drank type of chick. She merely served one purpose: entertainment. Like the many other women Marcus dealt with, Shaunte was cute and sexy. She had a small waistline, spread hips, and a fat curvaceous ass. It seemed all his women fit this physical description, but in different flavors. What set Niecey apart from most of them was her intellect and her disinterest in Marcus's street status and wealth. Despite all the women's differences, the end result remained the same, sexual pleasure at the end of the night. With Niecey though, Marcus took his time and was more passionate in the bedroom.

During the course of their conversation on the phone, Marcus found himself getting caught up in one of Sylvia's famous lectures.

"You know Shalonda brought the baby over last weekend," she stated, referring to Peaches. "I tried calling you because he kept asking about you. When the last time you been to see him?"

"I had 'em wit me a couple weeks ago." Marcus lied, trying to ease back from the discussion.

"Baby I'm telling you, that little boy needs you around him more," she warned. "He be around nothing but females who spoil him all the time. That's why he be acting so sensitive." Marcus knew Peaches had been in his mother's ear by her tone.

"I know, Ma, I know." He replied in hopes of cutting the topic short, but to no avail.

"Yeah, you always say 'I know, I know'. You need to start doing it!"

He respectfully accepted the mild bashing coming from his mother as he cruised around the city in his platinum blue Escalade with one of his dime pieces. Marcus said very little in return, not wanting to blow his high from the good weed smoke that he and Shaunte had in rotation.

Sylvia began informing Marcus on different family member's wellbeing. Marcus cared less about hearing issues concerning certain loved ones, but one person who was brought up struck a nerve.

"Momma been asking about you lately. She say you don't call and check up on her no more."

"She knows I love her to death," Marcus sorrowfully replied.

"I talked to her yesterday. She been complaining about having a bad cough lately."

"It ain't nuttin' too serious, is it?" Marcus asked with major concern.

"I don't know. She says it's been getting worse. I told her she needs to put them damn cigarettes down, but she won't listen to me. I set her up a doctor's appointment for next week so she could get checked out," Sylvia said while drawing alertness from her son. Grandma Emma had been a chain smoker since the age of 12 and at the age of 60 she wasn't planning on stopping for nobody.

After a couple seconds of an awkward silence, Sylvia could feel the worrying building in her son.

"Hello."

"Yeah, I'm here," Marcus muttered. He was obviously feeling guilty for not giving his beloved grandmother the attention she craved out of him.

"Baby, don't worry ya'self about it. She'll be okay. All I'm saying is jus' call her from time to time to check up on her. Even though she'll never admit it, everybody knows you her favorite gran'baby," Sylvia laughed out. "That lady cannot stop asking about you. Hell, I don't know why."

Marcus couldn't deny being his Granny's favorite. She loved all of her grandkids dearly, but when it came to Marcus she showed love that the other grandchildren couldn't grasp.

Before ending the call, Marcus sincerely vowed to change his behavior towards the two most important women in his world. As he continued to navigate through different blocks on the West Side his mind was cluttered with regretful thoughts. He couldn't imagine living his life without those two women.

"Everything okay, baby?" Shaunte asked while gently rubbing his inner thigh, sensing the emotional distress forming within Marcus after the phone conversation. Shaunte honored Marcus's street status to the fullest and was extremely loyal the small role she played in his movie called life.

After not getting a response out of him and seeing that he was in deep thought she didn't force the issue.

With her full, luscious, ruby red colored lips that were glossed up to perfection, Shaunte simply stated, "Well, if you need to talk about it I'm here for you." She said with sincerity but at the same time seductively. Despite thinking about how his current position in the mob had him neglecting the family that loved him the most, Marcus couldn't resist the slanted, Chinese-like eyes of Shaunte's that turned him on even more when she was high. Shaunte was one of those sexy, gutter chicks that kept a long expensive weave and had a body that looked as if it was sculpted together. She was fine as hell and any hood rich nigga would easily wife her, but to Marcus she was merely a chick on the side.

As they continued to ride, Marcus loosened up and kept on with his daily plan. Times when Marcus would put his life into perspective, positive thinking always seemed to deviate from his mindset due to the high demand his street status induced.

"Mr. Malone, lately there have been way too many unsolved murders in the Lawndale community. Sooner or later someone is gonna have to 'fess up to them. I have all these hypocritical community leaders demonstrating at 'Stop the Violence' rallies in the streets and they want answers!" Alderman Emanuel Davis scolded.

"Listen, all I done for the neighborhood over the years seems to be getting overlooked. The Save the Kids Foundation, all your funky ass fundraisers, who the hell was there to sponsor all that shit, me!" Big C harshly replied while sitting in one of the Alderman's secret locations in the west suburbs. These types of meetings never got leaked out to the public and especially not to either of their peers.

"Don't give me that shit! You know good-n-damn well you committed those acts for your own good!" the Alderman said. "I helped you clean up millions of dollars of blood money through these organizations! I helped you legalize your name so that you could live lavishly in those mansions you own!" The Alderman spoke with a sense of enmity, throwing all the favors he'd done in Big C's face.

"You need to watch your tone of voice," Big C warned.

As if Big C said nothing, Alderman Davis fearlessly kept on with his speech.

"Yeah, I must admit, you helped boost my popularity amongst my colleagues and all the law abiding citizens of the community by helping me take down some of the biggest drug lords this side of town have seen," the Alderman spoke out, revealing Big C's involvement with the law. "But again, that was another act of you saving your own ass from indictments."

Big C was getting agitated. He knew the Alderman had him on a string from all of his past street endeavors. Even though Big C was running his street business through Marcus these days, all that he'd done in the past was enough to put him under the penitentiary.

"It's been over five years since you helped us land that prominent case against Mr. Alphonso Smith. And hell, that was just a slap on the wrist," Alderman Davis said in a modest tone, referring to the arrest of Smitty.

"Don't you think it's about time you greased my palms again," he said before taking a sip out of his coffee mug.

With an evil glare in his eye, Big C slowly turned away and headed for the door. He was halfway out of the door when he was stopped in his tracks when the older black Alderman yelled with a mischievous grin covering his face, "Hey! Do the right thing Malone."

"Fuck you!" Big C shot back angrily before leaving out and slamming the door behind him.

Big C choices were limited. If he refused to cooperate, Alderman Davis would more than likely send the Fed's, DEA, and any other secret agents he had in pocket come after him. It was because of the Alderman that Big C had been safe in the past. Big C had the power to have the Alderman murdered at any given time, but he knew it would open up a can of worms.

Marlin had two blocks off Cermak pumping just as hard as any of the blocks around the Holy City. Since Marcus became Chief, he put each one of his childhood friends in great positions. Unlike the others, Marlin was more hands on with his two blocks. Marlin was always the grinder of the crew. If you ever needed to find him, all you had to do was look on whatever block he was working. He gave all of his personal guys the proper freedom they needed to prosper in the streets. From all the years they been around each other and all the struggles they overcame together, they all showed a certain loyalty towards one another that was indisputable.

By Marlin being so active on the blocks that he governed, he ran across a new product that many hustlers in the city didn't have access to in the nineties, hydro a.k.a. 'dro. Hydro was a much higher grade of weed from the mid-grade that people in the neighborhood were familiar with.

Marlin stumbled across his 'dro connect in an unusual fashion. One of his loyal dope customers, a young Jewish college student, exchanged a bag of weed for a blow and insisted one of the workers on Lawndale present it to Marlin. Because Marlin was always close around the area, he was able to get the package before any mishaps. He smoked a blunt of the red haired, crystal frosted 'dro with a couple of the Lords from off the block. They got so high from the good weed smoke that Marlin made it his business to catch up with his longtime customer. Like clockwork, the young fiend and a few of his college associates came back to purchase more blows before the day was over. Marlin approached him with a rundown of questions about the most potent marijuana he had ever inhaled. When it was all said and done, Marlin learned he was dealing with a mad scientist. Not only did the nerdy college kid have access to pounds, he also was the manufacturer. Instead of robbing his new prospect, like a typical small time street punk, he befriended him. Needless to say, both parties began to flourish over time. Marlin was getting pounds of hydro for dirt cheap when other guys around the city could barely get their hands on such a product.

Similar to how Marcus was the first to bring the mid-grade to the 'hood, he now had some 'reefa that was sure to become the wave of the future.

Marlin had Millard Street, a side block off Cermak, pumping like never before with miniature glass jars of good smelling, lime green, white frosted 'dro. Each jar contained 1.5 grams of the leafy plant for $25. Marlin had traffic flowing through his block like traffic jams during rush hours downtown. The 'dro was beginning to produce just as much as all of the surrounding dope infested blocks.

Marcus respected Marlin's hustle instead of stepping on his toes or pulling a power move like most Chiefs would have done once they saw a lot of money being made and knowing they weren't the supplier.

From the beginning of that summer to the end of the '99, Millard Street was the talk West Side amongst all the big timers who smoked heavily, for having a new and improved grade of weed that gave people a high that they had never experienced from weed smoke.

Chapter 21

A new year came, which also marked a new millennium. Rico's reign on the South Side was becoming epic. All it took was him making an example out of a couple of misfits that everyone in that area feared.

With about 30 Lords in attendance, some from out West and the others from off 115th Street, the new area Rico set out to conquer, they witnessed their leader recite parts of the Nation's law while in the midst of torturing two unruly perpetrators.

"My brothas, what we have in front of us is two niggas that couldn't abide by law," he said calmly while rubbing his hands together and pacing in circles around the brutally beaten, butt naked victims whom sat helpless in an abandoned basement on 115th and Eggleston.

They were slumped over in chairs unconscious and restrained by rope with clear plastic bags tightly covering their bloody mugs. They were unable to respond as Rico continued to speak, "These two mothafuckas obviously forgot the law of the land..." he paused and glanced around at his new recruits from out South. "...Law of Allah, take not life, which Allah have made sacred, except by way of justice and law. The law of our land...we cut off the hands of people who steal...for people who lie to Chiefs, we cut out tongues." Rico quoted in a horrific tone as he strolled towards a nearby hammer and a few rusted nails. Most of the crowd was on edge in fear of Rico's next move.

In complete silence, Rico walked up and slowly placed a nail that was as long as a finger onto the confined hand of the victim. The young Lords that weren't accustomed to such vicious acts reluctantly looked on as he pulled the hammer back like a handyman at work.

SPLAT!!! Rico slammed the hammer down on the nail with force, causing a gush of dark red blood. The young sufferer let out a muffled scream as the excruciating pain helped him regain to his consciousness. Moments later Rico turned to his side and reenacted the malicious act, getting the same response out of the other victim.

He stood there with a crazed look on his face watching the blood flow from both their hands with a sense of enjoyment. After a few moments Rico demonically instructed, "Take these clowns and put 'em up for later. I ain't through wit'em."

A couple of Shorties assertively took out the order while Rico turned to face the tense crowd, sensing fear in some and cold hearts in others. After forcefully tossing the hammer aside, Rico and his key enforcers paced out of the basement door with an electrifying aura surrounding them. Everyone that witnessed the incident knew that Rico meant business and was ready to prove their worth. Most of the Lords off 115th didn't have the heart and guts to take on such neighborhood terrorist. Once word got around that Rico was behind their disappearance, his name started ringing bells everywhere in the Wild Hunits. Anyone that claimed VL in the Hunits made it their business to pay Rico a visit.

Rico's IVL mob was growing by the masses on the South side after the demonstration. Kidnapping and torture was Rico's cup-of-tea so an act like this was normal for him.

Even though Rico's power was escalating in the Wild Hunits and his followers looked at him solely as their leader, he still taught them the right way. Rico made them aware of Marcus's Chief status with the Nation and through long distance communication, he illustrated Smitty as the overseer.

After so long, Rico had a hold on 115th and had most of the area claiming VL, even making some of the opposition convert over. Rico appointed his own officials to run the 'hood once people became aware of his status. On the outside looking in, Rico seemed to be the number one man for the IVL mob. He took it all in like a seasoned vet while staying loyal to Smitty, who had setup the mission to intrude out South without Marcus's consent. Smitty was secretly molding Rico into a feared and well rounded leader while keeping their direct connection discreet amongst other leaders in the Nation, including Marcus and Big C.

Chapter 22

After leaving from a hardnosed practice late in the evening, Chris and his two best friends did some joyriding through different 'hoods on the West Side. While keeping track of his curfew time, Chris and his buddies conversed on different topics but one in particular intrigued them the most...girls!

"Guess who I was on the phone wit' all last night?" Dante blurted out to Chris from the back seat as they accelerated through the gloomy streets.

"I ain't got time to be playin' no guessin' game, who?" Chris mildly replied as he leaned back in his seat with a certain cockiness as he drove down Lake Street underneath the El tracks.

"I was onna' phone wit' Kim and she had ya' girl Bridget on three way wit' us," Dante said, referring to Chris's first puppy love. Chris's virginity was broken in the sixth grade, at the early age of eleven, by none other than Bridget.

"That ain't my girl. She old news to me, I done moved on to bigger and better things."

"By the way she was talkin', I could tell she still got feelings for you-n-shit."

"Why you say that?" Chris asked curiously, loving the fact that one of his old flings was being mentioned.

"I'm sayin', all last night she kept askin' me questions bout'chu'. Who you fuckin' wit'? Do you still ask about her? You know, shit like that. We called you a couple times but'chu ain't answer."

"Yeah, I was on some'nt last night. I couldn't get to my phone, if you know what I mean." Chris emphasized excitedly while grabbing hold to his crotch area.

As they rotated through different blocks, the two continued their general teenage conversation concerning females while Randy sat quietly on the passenger side with his mind deeply drawn to the lyrics coming from Jigga. It seemed as though something detrimental was on his mind which was unusual coming from him. Chris took it upon himself to raise the issue.

"Randy, what the hell wrong wit'choo, man? You been quiet as hell ova' there."

"Shit." Randy quickly shot back, obviously shunning his two road dawgs off.

"Man, jo, you kno' how dude get when he ain't got nuttin' to smoke," Dante blurted out, showing no signs of pity. The two of them stayed at each other's throats but at the same time they had each other's back to the fullest.

"That's what'chu trippin' on? You ain't had no smoke in'nem lungs?" Chris asked lightheartedly.

"Hell naw," Randy snapped. "Weed don't make me, nigga! I told you 'bout listenin' to this lame. He don't be knowin' what the fuck he talkin' 'bout." That last comment was all it took to set off a squabble between the two.

For the remainder of the ride, the two went at each other without Chris being able to get a word in. Showing no patience for the back and forth arguing, Chris cut the joyriding short and took the expressway directly to the area they lived in.

When Chris got at the Central Avenue exit, Dante knew he was going to be the first to be dropped off since his apartment building was located seconds from the e-way.

"A'ight Jo, I'ma hit'chu up later on tonight," Dante said while prepping his exit. As Chris maneuvered out of the two lane traffic, pulling into a double park in front of the building, Dante added fuel to the fire before stepping out, "Chris, you need to holla' at this nigga. Maybe you could talk some sense into that big ass head." Dante playfully muffed Randy in the back of the head before racing out the car, not giving him time to retaliate.

Randy's household structure was slightly different than his counterparts. He shared space with four younger siblings in a single parent home. Some nights their mouths had to get fed before him and his mother's. Randy was feeling the pressure of becoming the breadwinner of the family at an early age. The welfare and SSI checks were the only income coming through. At times, that was hardly

125

enough to make ends meet. Seemingly embarrassed by the cards that life dealt him, Chris was the only person he would open up to about his personal situations.

Randy's mother stayed only ten minutes from Dante, so Chris headed in that direction with no questions asked. Minutes into driving down Central, Randy's true feelings began to boil over.

"Aey Chris, I ain't goin' over Sheryl house tonight," Randy said, referring to his mother by her first name. Staring deep off in space he continued to say. "Drop me off on my Gran'ma block."

Giving off an strange expression toward his friend's request, Chris pleaded, "This late? It's already eight o'clock." Although it wasn't too late, the sky was pitch black, showing only a full moon in the bitter coldness. Since it was mid-February, winter night hours often made it feel dreary outside and it seemed the hustlers and dope fiends were usually the only occupants on most inner city blocks.

"Chris, maaaann..." Randy hesitated while shaking his head in disgust. "I'm sick and tired of comin' in every night hearin' my lil' brothas and sistahs cryin' to me about they hungry and I cain't do a damn thane about it! You kno' I be tryna' do the right thing but that shit jus' ain't workin' for me. I gotta start makin' some moves...and a petty ass nine to five ain't gone cut it!"

Chris let his best friend have the floor as he continued to cruise towards his house. Chris had no intentions on changing his route. If anything, he was going to make an attempt to persuade his homey not to go on dangerous grounds.

"Yeah I feel you, but'chu kno' how hot it is on 21st, 'dem niggas stay into some shit ova' there. My brotha' jus' told me the other day to stay my ass from ova' that way." Chris said in hopes of convincing his friend to change his mind.

"Ain't shit safe these days, Chris." He countered while pleading his case, "I been fuckin' round on that block all my life, I'm used to 'dat shit."

"To be honest wit'chu, man, I'on even feel comfortable drivin' through there. That's how fucked up it is." Chris explained, inching closer to Randy's crib. "If you need some bread, I got'chu." Chris said as he reached toward his pocket to pull out a stack, trying everything in his power to help.

Marcus kept his little brother with a bankroll. Chris often got rewarded for doing the right thing.

Reaching over to stop Chris from going into his pocket, Randy replied, "Nah, nah, it ain't all about that. I 'preciate it, but temporary help ain't what I need. See Chris, I ain't got no older brotha' or a father to take care of us," he sentimentally stated, trying his hardest not to sound envious as he steadily spilled out emotions. "I gotta be that nigga...and from this point on, that's what I'ma do!"

At the age of sixteen, Randy was a late bloomer when it came to the hustling game. Being on 21st most of his life influenced his affiliation with the Lords. Playing sports was what kept him from being fully committed to the block, but his hoop dreams were slowly deflating.

Chris refused to deny his friend from providing for his family, even though he disagreed with the way he was going about getting it done. After pulling up to a red light at the next main street, Chris reluctantly made a right turn and headed east on Jackson, detouring directly towards the trenches.

Throughout the entire ten minute ride towards the Lawndale community, Chris tried everything in his power to talk his friend out of making a bad choice.

Turning off Homan onto the 21st strip was like warping into a ghost town. Despite a few stragglers, there wasn't a familiar face insight. Chris was sure his partner's frame of mind would change after not seeing the usual traffic flow on the strip. Cruising down the block Randy's grandmother lived on was like night and day compared to the strip. The regulars were out there operating the block like an organized, legit corporation. The moment Chris hit the block it was like a spark lit up inside Randy.

"Aey Chris, pull up to the middle of the block so I can see who all out here." He excitedly instructed while sitting up at attention trying to see who he could see.

Studying every car that drove through, the shorties on the block instantly recognized Chris' Regal gliding down the street with his 18 inch chrome Ateva's gleaming. Before Chris could come to a complete stop, some of the guys that were more acquainted with the two ran up and boldly intruded the car.

"Chris whudd up wit'chu Lord!" One of the shorties opened the driver's side door to shake up with Chris while the others forced Randy out of the passenger side.

"'Yo brotha' rode through here earlier in that new BMW truck; that mothafucka' right!" the young Lord exclaimed.

Marcus was unpredictable when it came to being noticed. When the streets became accustomed to seeing him in a certain vehicle he switched up in a heartbeat. In this case, Chris was in the blind about his brother newest toy, but he played it off as if he knew.

Even though it was below 20 degrees, Chris kept his door ajar and formally spoke to everyone that was out on the block. With only a Pelle Pelle leather jacket on and no hat to cover his head, he wasn't nearly equipped enough to stand out in the frigid weather. Everyone else that stood outside had on typical hustling attire, Carhart coats with the matching thermal hoodie underneath or triple goose bubble coats with the fur trimmed hoods.

In the midst of Chris speaking his peace, the few that stood around his car spoke out on different issues all at once.

"Aey Lord, you kno' Marlin got that 'dro out here. Ma'fucka's been buyin' the hell outta' that shit. I got'a blunt rolled up right now, let's bend'a few blocks and smoke one." One of the misfits

129

recommended in hopes of being seen with the promising hoop star. Withstanding the peer pressure, Chris replied, "Nah, not right now. I got somewhere to be. I'a slide back through here to fuck wit'chall." Chris fabricated, already feeling uneasy from being double parked on the block for too long.

"...You talkin' to a real superstar right there. He ain't got time for the bullshit..." one of the bystanders blurted out from afar in a joking manner. Before pulling all the way off, Randy flagged Chris down and made his way to the car. Chris cracked his door open once again.

"'Preciate you my nigga," said Randy as he shook up with his partner. "Here go a jar of that 'dro, courtesy of Lord." Randy dropped the jar in his hand and pointed over to whom it came from. Chris chucked the deuce showing gratitude for the hand out, which came from one of the Lords that ran the night shift.

By Chris being the younger brother of a Chief, he was automatically labeled as one of their own. Chris never denied being part of the Lords and whenever he would come around the old neighborhood everyone in the streets, from young to old, showed him nothing but love on the strength of Marcus.

Chris managed to go on about his business. Talking to the guys out on the block boosted his adrenaline and made him feel more at ease about dropping Randy off at his grandmother's house, who he had no interest in going to see after getting situated with the other hustlers.

Chris ended up enjoying a personal smoke session on his long, dreadful hour and a half trip to their south suburb estate.

Marcus pulled up on 19th and Hamlin in his newly bought midnight blue, peanut butter colored interior 2000 BMW X5. He was meeting up with Steve on their old block. The house now was used as one of his stash spots.

On this sunny, winter morning Marcus was ready to present Steve with some mind boggling news. As he walked up to the truck, Steve's facial expression made it obvious that he was every bit surprised at Marcus's new toy.

After hopping in, the smell of new car leather and Armani fragrance instantly took hold of Steve's nostrils. Marcus's class level had escalated tremendously since he first got in the game. Steve was an admirer of how Marcus handled himself while being in such a high seat for the mob.

"Gaddamn, this how we doin' it now..." Steve said jokingly as they dapped each other up. Marcus gave a slight smirk from Steve's remark. "Buyin' new BMW trucks-n-shit wit' out lettin' nobody kno'." He said all this while glancing throughout the luxury of the SUV. This was the first year BMW trucks were introduced and Marcus was the first street nigga on the West Side with one. Steve, on the other hand, wasn't short stopping by pulling up in a '98 teal green Ford Excursion.

"Yeah, I jus' grabbed this ma'fucka boutta' week ago," Marcus replied in a modest and humble tone. "I sold the Escalade to one of Kunta's business partners. That nigga offered me ninety thousand cash for it wit' no hesitation. I had to let it go." Marcus had been getting good money for a while without any major mishaps, but his name still wasn't legit. Kunta helped him purchase expensive things.

"You kno' yo' momma gon' trip out when she see this, right? She already think you be spendin' all your money on unnecessary shit."

"I kno'. I already thought of a script to hit her wit'." Marcus replied as they both laughed at the thought of how feisty Sylvia could get when it came down to her loved ones. Being grown and deep in the streets never stopped Marcus from valuing his mother's advice. Sylvia often stressed him about changing his life and cleaning his money through legitimate businesses. She even took it upon herself to take accounting and real estate classes in hopes of helping her first born see a better future. Sylvia knew if she came up with a lucrative investment plan, Marcus would be all in without a shadow of a doubt.

In the course of discussing other family matters, Marcus went directly to street business. Without any introduction he handed Steve a folded up piece of paper.

"What's this?" Steve asked with a half grin still covering his face.

While scanning through the words carefully, the happy grin that once covered his mug slowly formed into a concerned expression.

"Where the hell you get this from?!" He asked suspiciously while flipping the letter from front to back looking for a name.

"It was sent to me boutta' week ago. I been so busy lately I what'nt able to get up wit'chu when I first got it."

"Tell your pops to open his eyes---the disease right beside him..." He read the last sentence in the letter out loud with a strained expression as he tried putting context clues together. Having a good idea where the letter came from and who was being insinuated, Steve still asked, "Who sent it?"

"Smitty," Marcus replied boldly, looking Steve square in the eye.

Slowly shaking his head from side to side while studying the letter, it was obvious that Steve was recollecting his thoughts.

"Look Marcus, man," Steve said sounding like he was preparing himself to give a power speech. "I been knowin' Smitty for'a long time. One thing I know about dude, he stay plottin'. Now jus' think about it. C get knocked off, Smitty come home to the throne and own damn near the whole West Side through you. It won't be nobody that's active as powerful as him on this side of town, other than you."

Smoothly rubbing his goatee contemplating on what was being said, Marcus sat in silence and allowed Steve to talk. The body language coming from Marcus was nothing less than seriousness and Steve felt it.

"So what'chu tellin' me?" Marcus asked.

"I'm tellin' you to make the right move. Don't do nothin' you'a regret," Steve warned. "He is tellin' you to kill a Chief of Chiefs that's been having a tight grip on the mob for damn near 20 years. If you thinkin' about knockin' him off without extreme repercussion coming your way, then you need to think again." Steve spoke intensely forcing Marcus's undivided attention. "I kno' you honor Smitty and want to display your loyalty, but understand some'nt, being behind them walls make'a nigga have crazy thoughts. Believe me, I kno'," Steve said, acknowledging being locked up and in similar situations.

Reaching for the door handle Steve ended the conversation by stating, "Remember a long time ago I asked you did you kno' what'chu was getting' ya'self into. It's a dirty game, jack. You cain't trust nobody these days." Steve shook his head with pity before stepping out of the truck.

As he left Marcus's presence, Steve couldn't help but to put the situation into prospective. There was no way he could disregard Big C's involvement with the law, especially after he revealed being the trigger man behind the murder of Marcus's ole man, something that was also kept from Steve for years. It took everything in his power not to tell Marcus his father's killer was the topic of discussion the time he walked in on them. Steve knew if he broke the news, Marcus emotions would've taken control and that very well could've been dangerous to both parties. Instead of stirring up strife, Steve took it upon himself to start his own private investigation on the person whom he helped protect for so many years.

Chapter
24

It had been nearly a year since Marcus and Niecey started being intimate with each other and things were beginning to heat up. Niecey was the type that demanded her respect from the men she dated and Marcus was no exception. She was the first woman Marcus ever considered being in a serious relationship with since becoming grown.

Because of his high ranked status Marcus was very recognizable amongst his peers. This prohibited him from appearing in a lot of public places. In most cases acknowledgments would come from people he didn't really know, which could be dangerous because his status always made him a target.

Because Niecey was not totally aware of Marcus's street credibility, she was naïve to the reasons why he preferred to be more private. She convinced him to tag along with her on an afternoon of shopping at one of the city's most exquisite malls, the Water Tower located on Michigan Avenue also known as the Magnificent Mile, in the heart of downtown Chicago.

They walked through seven different floors for hours. Passing through some of the most expensive stores was taking a toll on Marcus and every minute that went by he let it be known.

"Niecey, I kno' damn well you ain't fenna' go in that sto' again!" Marcus expressed with disbelief as they stopped in front of Lord & Taylor, both hands filled with different shopping bags.

"I know, baby, I know," she sympathized while reaching up to peck him on the cheek. "I promise it'll only take a sec."

"Yeah right. You been sayin' that since we got here." Marcus complained with a sense of humor. "Look, while you in there, I'ma sit my black ass down somewhere and relax." Niecey's body language spoke volumes as she watched him walk away. She was turned on by Marcus's mischief.

Instead of settling down after seeing Denise comfortably browsing in the store Marcus eased his way to a nearby jewelry store.

Since The Water Tower was so upscale and predominantly occupied by older, wealthy business people Marcus was automatically noticed and stereotyped by the European jeweler.

"Hello sir, may I help you?" He voiced his discontent in a thick accented English after noticing Marcus was focused on a particular piece.

"Yes you can as a matter of fact," Marcus shot back, matching the salesman's harsh tone. "Let me check out that women's tennis bracelet."

"Are you referring to the Anjolee Double Diamond X Link?" The jeweler elegantly asked looking surprised at his selection while unlocking the glass case. Marcus showed a disturbed expression at the comment as the salesman continued to present the bracelet.

"This bracelet has a total of two carats of diamonds, which means it could be a bit pricey. Now, we do have the Anjolee Classic Diamond Link for a much more reasonable price. If I'm not mistaking it was recently marked down. Would you be interested in that one instead, sir?" Before Marcus could respond the jeweler headed towards the other bracelet.

Looking down at the $1600 price tag, Marcus stopped the salesman in his tracks.

"Excuse me, that won't be necessary. I'll take this one."

"Really?" The salesman stated shocked as he turned to face Marcus.

"Yes, really," Marcus replied hastily. "Now, if it's not a problem I would like it gift wrapped."

Once the jeweler saw Marcus pull out a neatly folded, thick knot of cash from his pocket he began performing better customer service. As he snapped the rubber band and peeled off sixteen crisp, one hundred dollar bills Marcus stated, "You shouldn't judge every book by its cover."

"Oh, sir, I'm sorry if there was any misunderstanding."

"You know what, don't worry 'bout it," Marcus interrupted irritably. "Jus' gimme my receipt so I can get the hell up outta' here." He tossed the money on the counter as if it was nothing and the fearful salesman put a rush on Marcus's order while attempting to explain his rude approach.

As they departed the mall's parking garage in Niecey's cream GS 300 Lex bubble, Marcus sat on the passenger side and directed the way. Denise very well thought they were headed back towards the far south suburbs, but she was soon detoured to a much closer destination.

"Baby, shouldn't we have turned right on Ontario to get to the expressway?" She asked as she turned onto Wabash off of Michigan Avenue.

"Trust me, I got this." He said while directing her towards his low-key condo that was located off of Congress and Dearborn. Marcus never exposed Denise to any of his spots around the city, only the family home.

Pulling into a parking space in front of a three story loft, she had no idea where Marcus was taking her. Developing such an intimate relationship with Marcus over the months forced her to drop all guards, causing her to become more comfortable while being in his presence. In other words, wherever they were headed she was content with it, knowing how spontaneous Marcus could be.

As they walked through the decorative and luxurious lobby, the young and hip doorman made his way around the front desk to acknowledge Marcus as he pressed for the elevator. The doorman always greeted Marcus differently from the other wealthy tenants. He always tried hard to show Marcus how hipped to the game he was, but in all actuality Marcus viewed him as a square.

Marcus and Denise were tripping out on the obnoxious doorman as they got off on the 18th floor. As Marcus led her through his front door, Niecey's train of thought shifted.

"Wow!" She exclaimed after a glimpse around the condo. "Definitely a bachelors pad, but nice." She complimented while scoping around the apartment, noticing that the place was half furnished. With only a 62 inch Sony HD floor model TV, two royal blue velvet pull out couches, a five disk CD changer hanging along the wall, and a mini bar filled with a variety of liquors, it was obvious that this was one of Marcus's player pads.

"Make ya'self comfortable." Marcus stated after flicking on the track lights and heading towards the kitchen.

Taking him up on his offer, Denise began undoing her scarf and coat.

"You can't possibly come here a lot."

"Why you say that?" He questioned while getting the proper utensils he needed to relax the mood.

"It's extremely neat around here. I know you're not cleaning up like this."

Leaving the kitchen with two custom designed wine glasses and a bottle of Pinot Grigio, Marcus's intentions were definitely to lighten up the mood. Impressed by his wine selection Denise blurted out, "You remembered what type of wine to get?"

"Yeah, what'chu think I'on be payin' attention?"

"Most young guys have short attention spans. No offense." Niecey had Marcus by a couple of years so she often joked about him being younger than her.

"Remember I told you, I ain't like most other guys." Marcus assured as they tipped glasses. He reached over to grab the remote to the CD changer and pressed play. Soon the smooth sounds of Keith Sweat came pumping out of the speakers a real mood setter.

Reminiscing on the classic seemed to strike a nerve in Niecey as she began to passionately sing the beginning lyrics, "How deep is your love...how deep is your love! Uh uuhhh, that's my jaaaamm! What you know about that?" She stated with spunk, questioning Marcus's taste in good music. Little did she know Marcus had an old soul. He grew up around a family full of city slickers, pimps with silky smooth conversations, and heartless gangsters who killed when it was necessary.

Though the atmosphere was set on chill mode, the wine combined with mixed emotions slowly turned a seductive conversation into real talk. Marcus closed the small space that separated the two. Before Marcus could fully take it to the next level, something they both were used to, Niecey stopped all movements.

"Look, Marcus..." she said, showing signs of a sensual sensation as Marcus nibbled on her ear. "I can't fake this anymore, baby. We need to talk." She eased back from his warm embrace.

"We need to talk?" This was the first time Niecey had shown resistance toward him. In the past, whenever Marcus showed signs of needing some sexual healing, she never deprived him of it. Once Marcus saw the seriousness on her face, he settled his libido and conducted himself in a more mature manner.

"Okay then, cool, let's talk."

Respecting Niecey's wishes, Marcus arose from the couch, sat his glass on the nearby wood framed, glass coffee table and allowed her to speak.

"Marcus, I tried to avoid having this conversation for a long time now, but I can't continue to go on like this."

"Go on like what? Talk to me." He stated, showing signs of being agitated.

"I mean, what're we doing? We been seeing each other for a year now and I still don't fully understand where we stand. I'm saying, are we in a committed relationship or are we jus' together when it's convenient for you?"

Marcus took a deep breath before diving into the conversation. This was the first time he truly cared about how a woman felt. In most cases, Marcus would tell a female what they wanted to hear, but there was something special about Niecey that made him feel obligated to reveal his true feelings.

"Niecey, baby look, I ain't never been in'a serious committed relationship before. This prob'le the longest I ever been wit' one woman." Marcus said while looking her directly in the eye.

"And why is that?" she asked searching for answers.

"This life I live won't allow me to commit."

"And what type of life is that," she quickly shot back, only to get a bold stare from Marcus. "I mean, I'm not stupid. I kno' you'a hustler," she said with sarcasm as if a secret was revealed. "Is this all you plan on doin' for the rest of your life?"

Being asked about his street life by a female made Marcus feel uncomfortable. The other women he dealt with were familiar with his reputation in the streets so they knew what they were up against.

"I plan to get out one day," Marcus retorted, showing little interest in having the conversation.

"Marcus, I don't think you fully understand how I really feel about you," Denise said, making an attempt to lay everything out on the line. She became emotional and tears came to her eyes as she explained, "I look at you as someone I could have a future with...I'm just afraid of having my heart broken due to something tragic happening to you."

Sitting there listening to Niecey made Marcus consider his feelings towards her. Looking into her eyes Marcus could see Denise had given a lot of thought to their situation. Everything she said was heartfelt but the fact still remained, Marcus was a Chief over one of the original branches of the VL Nation, there was no way he could up and turn away from that without paying with his life. Marcus was the anchor to feeding a lot of niggas. Without him flooding majority of the blocks on the West Side with the best dope in the city, most joints wouldn't have been as lucrative.

Marcus wanted to keep it real with Denise by all means. He didn't feel the need to mislead her even if it meant losing her.

"Niecey, I'a be lyin' if I told you I could jus' stop what I'm doin' ova' night," Marcus said.

"Baby I'm not asking---"

"Hold on a'minute, let me finish," Marcus cut her short, letting it be known who was still in control. "You the type of woman a man needs in his corner. I would hate to lose you, but I rather see you living your life happy even if it's not wit' me."

"Marcus, baby, can you at least promise me you'll try to make a change?" Denise asked sincerely. Even though Denise was an independent, strong minded young lady, it was obvious that her heart had been captivated by Marcus's charm and stability. At times, his flamboyant lifestyle intrigued her, though she'd never admit it.

Marcus sat quietly staring in her face, admiring every detail that made her beautiful. He realized Niecey's potential and how she could possibly help his transition to a legitimate lifestyle. Niecey instantly pulled closer and softly caressed his face and repeated her previous question.

"Baby... Promise me?" She asked sentimentally. Still not getting a response out of Marcus, she wasted no time locking lips with him. She softly sucked his bottom lip, which eventually turned into intense kissing, Niecey reacted as though she couldn't resist him any longer.

Before they could go any further Marcus stated, "Awe, I almost forgot... I got'a lil' somen't for you." Marcus eased off the couch and headed towards the closet where their coats hung. Niecey sat there confused. not knowing what to expect.

"Here." Marcus handed her a long suede jewelry box before sitting down close to her. Niecey took her time and admired the wrapping, causing Marcus to blurt out, "Well, open it..."

The moment her eyes caught the sparkle from the two carat double diamond link bracelet, she began praising the gift and graciously thanking Marcus.

Marcus slowly began removing all of her clothing and kissed every inch of her body as the effects of the wine kicked into overdrive. Between the buzz from the wine and the sparks she felt from

Marcus's touch, Niecey knew this night was going to be a night she'd never forget.

25

Chris was running late for first period, as usual. Straggling through the doors of the school, he walked into an unexpected crowd standing around the student center. Instead of loud and unruly teenagers running around uncontrollably, everyone seemed to have long, sad faces. Most of the females were consoling one another while grieving.

With his clothes still reeking with marijuana from his routine early morning session, paranoia began to set in. Chris could feel tension in the air. Determined to see what everyone was so torn about, Chris headed straight to his normal social group.

"Wassup Jo," Chris walked up to one of his fellow teammates and shook up with him. "What the fuck erybody 'round here lookin' all crazy for?" Chris asked, noticing how his guys weren't as excited to see him as they normally would be.

"Man, cuz..." Dante began to say looking down while shaking his head sorrowfully.

"Man cuz what?!" Chris slightly snapped at his friend's delay, sensing some type of bad news.

"The administrator jus' made an announcement over the P.A..." Dante hesitated with his eyes on the verge of tearing up. After gathering himself he was able to choke out, "Man...Randy dead!"

The shocking news left Chris dumbfounded and speechless. He didn't say a word as he listened to a few students who were standing around speculating on what happened.

"They say he was ova' on Christiana a'couple nights ago and some niggas jus' rode through dumpin'..."

"...I had a feeling somen't was wrong when he didn't show up to class or practice..." Another one of the teammates sadly stated.

Randy was the victim of a retaliation drive-by shooting the night Chris dropped him off. Out of all people that were out on the block that night he was the only one fatally shot. He died in the hospital two days later from four gunshot wounds to the back. It didn't seem odd that Chris hadn't heard from his friend in those couple days. It wasn't his first time being missing in action. Randy had one foot in the streets and never had his mind fully into school. His family structure was part of the reason his decision making was so poor. Without a male role model, Randy never had anyone in his ear to tell him right from wrong.

While everyone stood around mourning, Chris stormed out of the school doors like a mad man. A few of his friends tried running behind him to give him support but to no avail. Chris felt responsible to say the least. If he only followed his first mind and dropped Randy off at home he would have still been alive. The entire ride Chris had a bad feeling about Randy going on 21st, but he allowed himself to be convinced. Chris could hardly believe the news that was just laid on him. He left school and headed straight to Randy's mother's house to get a better understanding of his best friend's murder. Besides Marcus getting shot up, this was the only other time Chris ever felt empty and disgusted. He was starting to realize the street life wasn't as glamorous and easy as Marcus and Steve made it look at times.

Since reading the letter sent to Marcus from Smitty, Steve began contemplating on his Chief's loyalty to the mob. Within the 20 years that Steve had been under Big C, he had never once seen any flaw in his leadership. Although there were times where he disagreed on certain decisions that Big C made, he still went along with no questions asked. Steve was well aware of Big C's involvement with certain law officials that he kept on payroll, but never in his wildest dreams did he believe Big C would do anything to purposely endanger him or the Nation.

Steve took heed to the accusations that came from the joint concerning Big C. Since then he began lurking, trying to find out if there was any truth in what he had read. The few times he investigated and scoped out Big C's locations there was nothing out of the ordinary going on that showed that Big C was giving out valuable information.

Steve kept everything secretive by not telling Marcus and damn sure not making his spying obvious to his Chief. Nonetheless, Steve was determined to get to the bottom of the situation and continued to keep track of Big C's whereabouts.

One particular day after leaving Big C's presence Steve made it seem like he had things to attend to. Instead, he decided to secretly trail Big C. This day Big C led him to the west suburbs to a site Steve wasn't familiar with.

Sitting in a low-key silver Toyota Camry with dark tinted windows, Steve was parked where he couldn't be recognized. He noticed Big C enter a building that had no sign to reveal what the office was used for. After not seeing any movement coming in or out of the spot for a couple of hours Steve began to get impatient and was ready to pull out. Before he was able to do so a familiar face came walking out. Once Steve cast his eyes on the older white detective named Chronin, he immediately became alert. Chronin was a Colombo look-alike. Throughout the years of him being in the line of duty he had several murder attempts made on his life by some powerful organizations. If you were a made man making major noise in the streets, Chronin was the last person you wanted stalking your every move. He was famous for taking down plenty of mob Chiefs in his day. Steve wondered what business Big C could possibly have with such a slime. Instantly, Marcus came to the forefront of his thoughts.

Moments after seeing Chronin leave the office Steve witnessed Big C strolling out and to make matters worse, the most crooked Alderman in the city was leaving behind him, Emanuel Davis.

"Ain't this boutta' bitch...!" Steve frowned and cursed out loud. He was in a state of shock. He couldn't believe his eyes. He was witnessing his longtime Chief looking as if he was cooperating with the two individuals they strived so diligently to avoid for years. The meeting looked to be secretive and Steve didn't like what he had seen. He was now pondering thoughts on all the allegations coming from the past leaders who were now confined to penitentiary cells for years from Chronin's harsh investigations.

Watching the two get into separate cars before peeling out, Steve scrunched his eyes with fury. His expression showed his disappointment. Something had to be done and done quickly.

Steve let them drive out of sight before pulling off. He knew he had a lot to think about and little time to do so.

Chapter
26

Usually before Marcus's monthly pick up from Kunta they would have lunch together at a restaurant of Kunta's choice. This time was no different. Marcus met up with him downtown on Rush Street at an upscale steakhouse named Gibson's. Kunta was a regular at most five star eateries in the downtown area. Being Kunta's friend helped Marcus become well rounded. He was a street nigga with class an excellent combination.

Kunta was more than just a plug in Marcus's eyes. He also looked at him as a mentor. Marcus always talked to Kunta about personal and street situations. He valued his advice, figuring Kunta was out for his best interest.

Sitting in the dim and cozy elegant restaurant, they both ordered their favorite dish. Kunta had the baby spinach salad with hot bacon dressing followed by the eight ounce Australian lobster tail. Marcus on the other hand enjoyed the Seared Tuna Nicoise

Salad as an appetizer and the Double Lamb Chops as an entree.

Mostly small talk transpired while enjoying their appetizers. By the time the entrees arrived, Kunta brought up a more familiar subject.

"So, business been well?" he asked while cutting through his lobster tail. "I haven't heard from you since we last met."

"Well, ya' kno, the same ole bullshit. A loss here, a loss there. A few unsolved murders... nuttin' too major. I guess I can't complain." Marcus spoke with a sense of exhaustion while sipping on a glass of a white wine that costs $110 per bottle. Being around Kunta helped Marcus learn about different expensive wines which impressed the women with class that he was becoming accustomed to dating.

Whenever it came time for Marcus to re-up they always made it a full day affair. Since he brought Kunta over a million dollars in cash on a monthly basis, it was impossible for them to make quick transactions. They both had different low key condos in the downtown area, so they were able to switch up spots to count the money. The supplies were never in the same facility when counting money. Marcus always had J.R. and one other person on point to pick up the work wherever they decided to have it dropped off. This operation went smoothly every month.

In the midst of having a general conversation, Marcus brought up the predicament that he was put in.

"Yeah, man, I recently got'a kite sent to me from the joint," Marcus said while eating on his food. "Some serious shit goin' on that I got'a check out."

"Well, I'm sure it's nothin' that you cain't handle," Kunta replied.   He emphasized Marcus's ability to handle street business.   Kunta was very familiar with the two mob figures Marcus dealt with. He never got involved with the organizations, in fact, he'd rather not be seen and stay behind the scenes, distributing his endless supplies through Marcus. He knew Marcus had a unique position. Having full access to the West Side, especially amongst most VL's around the Holy City was unheard of.

"Have you been in touch with Smitty?" Kunta asked while focusing on enjoying his meal. "Shouldn't he be home soon?" He continued to ask questions before Marcus could reply.

"Yeah, I been fuckin' wit'em.   He'a be home in'a few years. That shit comin' up fast too."

"That's a good thing, right?! You should be happy!" Kunta stated joyfully in his strong foreign accent.

"I'on kno'. It depends on where his mind at. I mean, if he can't 'cept the fact that I'ma' keep doin me then we might have a problem." Marcus said with a more serious expression.

"Well, hopefully by that time you should have your business all the way intact, that way you won't have to deal with all the unnecessary bullshit. If he wants to take over the land, let him have it! You˙

come too far to lose your life over nonsense!" Kunta explained using a tone that showed he truly cared.

What Kunta failed to realize was that leaving the streets wasn't an easy task for Marcus. Because he was a young Chief, he hadn't put in enough years to retire. And even if he did the VL mob wouldn't have respected his decision. Marcus was the main source for a lot of the heads of the organization. If he left the game prematurely, they all would be struggling to find trustworthy connects. Giving up Kunta to the Nation was not an option for Marcus.

Still, Marcus contemplated other moves. Kunta always stressed to him the importance of putting money towards legal investments, but it seemed like this time Marcus really took heed to Kunta's advice.

Chapter
27

    Sylvia decided to have a rare get together out south for Grandma Emma's 61st birthday. It was the first of April and the weather had begun to break. The inconsistent spring like weather was now morphing into mild temperatures.

    Sylvia invited family members that Marcus didn't necessarily agree with coming to their house, but Sylvia's six siblings insisted on being with their mother for the special occasion. Out of Grandma Emma's seven children, six of them either had drug addictions or were content with living in poverty. Although she was the youngest, Sylvia was the only level minded person out of her two sisters and four brothers.

    Of course, most of the family didn't have transportation to get to the far south suburbs so Sylvia had to make a way for them. She spent majority of her day picking up family members. She even convinced Marcus, Steve, and Chris to escort some relatives that were scattered around the city to the house.

Sylvia was hoping to have a civilized time and enjoy her Mother's birthday without any disruptions. In the past, it seemed inevitable for some confusion to stir up when the Williams family got together. The backyard and parts of the mini-mansion was packed with the family. Sylvia made no exceptions to her rule about entering certain parts of the house. She allowed the kids to roam anywhere in the house except through her expensive living room. The only chance people got to see the showroom was when Sylvia gave a tour. Most of the family wasn't accustomed to being around expensive material things so Sylvia had to be strict.

Everyone seemed to be in their separate groups around the house. Grandma Emma and her older friends and siblings sat in the kitchen area reminiscing and eating the barbecue that Steve had prepared. Grandma Emma was trying her hardest to have a good time despite a terrible cough that the family couldn't ignore. Every time someone crossed her path showing concern for her health she would politely brush them off, light up another cigarette, and insist that she was doing fine. But watching her cough up globs of mucus with specks of blood every other minute told another story.

Marcus tried showing Niecey special attention but a select few family members were determined not to allow that to happen. Uncle Willie, in particular, had been a pest to Marcus since his younger days. Uncle Willie was the oldest out of the seven. Back in the day he was full-fledged in the pimping game and making good money. After getting strung out on heroin, all of that eventually came to a halt. A couple of missing teeth and a massive receding hairline didn't stop him from thinking he still had it though.

"Nephew, keep doin' ya' muthafuckin' thang. Don't let nobody tell you nuttin' different." He stated with a drunken slur, not giving much space between him and Marcus's ear. Uncle Willie followed Marcus and Niecey all the way from the backyard to the front. They stood on the circular driveway in front of the open garages listening to Uncle Willie's nonsense before Marcus interrupted.

"Ain't nobody heard from Uncle Winston?" Marcus asked about one of his other uncles who was missing in action.

"Naw, ain't seen the mothafucka since I loaned him a dub about a month ago. When I do catch 'em, I'ma kick his mothafuckin ass! Him and ya' Uncle Frank. They ain't shit but some gaddamn playa' haters. They always be talkin' shit about how you out here doin' wrong but be the first ones in ya' face beggin'. Fuck 'dem niggas. You kno' I always been the realest uncle you had on both sides of yo' family." Uncle Willie continued to speak out emotionally, displaying the effects of the cheap Thunderbird liquor that reeked through his pores.

"Aight Unk, I'ma' catch up wit'chu in'a minute." Marcus had had enough of the senseless talk. It wasn't long before Uncle Willie revealed his true motive.

"Nephew, let me spit-a-bug in ya' ear." Pulling Marcus aside, Uncle Willie proceeded to ask pitifully, "Let Unk hold a'couple dollas?" Marcus went into his pocket and pulled out a bank roll full of crisp hundreds and gave his uncle a one hundred dollar bill like it was nothing. Uncle Willie jetted out with a huge grin on his face while showing major gratitude.

All Marcus wanted to do was spend time with the important people in his life. Marcus was a family favorite on his mother's side of the family. When they had the chance, which was rare, certain one's tried clinging to him as long as they could only because they saw the dollar signs. Certain family members claimed to love him so much, but in all actuality, they cared less about his well-being and more about getting into his pockets.

After making it back inside, Marcus and Niecey settled in the kitchen area where Grandma Emma and a couple of others sat. All of the counters were filled to capacity with all kinds of food like barbecue chicken, rib tips, bratwurst sausages, hot dogs, corn on the cob, spaghetti, and potato salad. Steve took pride in using the grill. It didn't matter the weather, he would put a piece of meat on the grill in a heartbeat and was damn good at it.

With Niecey sitting by his side enjoying a plate he prepared, Marcus began conversing with his grandmother. Grandma Emma loved being in the presence of her grandkids, especially Chris and Marcus because they used to live in the same household. During the times when Sylvia juggled two jobs, Grandma Emma was their built-in care taker. So it was safe to say that Chris and Marcus had a distinctive closeness with their grandmother. unlike the others.

"Momma, you had enough to eat?" Marcus asked in the middle of piling his plate up with everything in sight.

After some excruciating coughs and spitting up in a nearby empty Pepsi can, Grandma Emma responded, "Yeah, bay, I tried eating a lil' somen't. Momma just ain't been having no appetite lately." Right after finishing her sentence she went into another coughing episode.

Fearful of his grandmother's condition Marcus promptly asked, "Momma what they say when you went to the doctor? Did they give something for that cough?" Marcus's concern and attention went directly towards his grandmother's health as he sat his food down and didn't bother to take a bite, despite his hunger.

"Baby, them damn doctors don't be knowin' what they talkin' about. They'll tell you one thing and it be another." She said all of this while taking deep breaths and slowly rubbing across her chest.

"Momma, you need to put them cigarettes down!" Marcus expressed himself more forcefully than usual.

Her best friend Grace spoke up and expressed her concern saying, "Baby, I been telling your grandmother them cigarettes ain't doing her any good. She just can't seem to stop!"

Grandma Emma rolled her eyes at Grace's statement, looking as if she was accustomed to hearing that come from her long time best friend.

"Lord have mercy, Marcus baby, sit down and eat your food shuga," Grandma Emma said in a tiresome tone while grabbing Marcus's hand and guiding him to a seat.

"Momma gon' be just fine. The good Lord will make sure of that." In between a nasty coughing spell she managed to ask, "Now where's that big head great gran'baby of mine at?" Grandma Emma was obviously trying to change the subject.

"He out there runnin' 'round somewhere." Marcus said as he began to nibble on his food, still not feeling at ease about his grandmother's condition.

"I'm glad to see you spending more time with him. That boy needs you in his life." With her hand resting on Marcus's free hand, she looked over at Niecey and said, "Honey, maybe with someone as fine as you by his side, we won't have to worry about him being out in them streets so much." She laughed, only to start up another coughing frenzy. Niecey humbly smiled at Grandma Emma's statement, as she hoped for the same out of Marcus. In the past, Marcus tried keeping his street endeavors away from his grandmother but his growing status and all the fast money that he was accumulating prohibited that from happening. After a while she realized her grandson was in too deep.

From then on, all she could do was pray for him and hope for a change.

Not entertaining what was previously said, Marcus stayed on the matter at hand. "Momma maybe you need to come stay out here so we could see about'chu betta'."

"Oooh no, baby, y'all stay too far out for Momma. I'll never be able to catch my bingo bus from way out here," she chuckled, clearly showing her love for bingo. Since Marcus could remember, Grandma Emma always had a passion for bingo buses and gambling boats. Besides smoking cigarettes, bingo and slot machines were the other things she didn't plan on giving up anytime soon.

As they continued to talk and eat, the coughing and spitting up carried on relentlessly. Marcus was worried about his grandmother and her continuous insistence that she was okay, which made him feel helpless. Once Sylvia and a few others stepped back into the kitchen area, they were determined to get her some help.

Sylvia quickly reacted to her mothers' illness when Emma became caught up in another devastating coughing frenzy.

"Momma this is ridiculous! We gotta get you to a hospital." Sylvia stated in a worrisome tone as she and others did everything in their power to try to soothe her cough.

Grandma Emma was still behaving stubbornly as all her kids and grandkids helped put on her shoes and jacket. She struggled to catch her breath after almost coughing her lungs out. Things got real intense and the family was in utter stillness thinking that something could be fatally wrong with the strong woman who had been the glue that held the family together for so many years

After everyone helped get Grandma Emma squared away in the car, Sylvia ordered Marcus to stay back at the house to make sure everyone left safely. It was obvious that the party was over as the minds of everyone that was left back at the house were on the condition of Grandma Emma. Once the house became settled, Marcus tried easing his mind with Niecey and his son MJ by his side.

On a record breaking 80 degree Friday afternoon in April, Marcus made a rare appearance on 21st and Homan. It was uncommon for Marcus to post up on the block these days. Some of the younger Lords that were new to the organization barely knew what he looked like. They only speculated or had seen him flying past in one of his expensive cars. They were more accustomed to seeing Peewee, who was a three star elite, and Lil G, who controlled the 21st strip. Still, they respected Marcus as their Chief.

There had been a few unsolved murders on the strip in the past few months. Instead of Marcus hearing about the news through the streets, he wanted to get a better feel of what was going on in person. He parked his BMW truck on Homan and before long, the strip was packed with IVL's that wanted to get a rare glimpse of the person who was the anchor behind the excellent dope that was out on the 21st strip causing all the hypes to flood the blocks.

Marcus's 5 foot 11 inch, 230 pound stature stood out significantly amongst the crowd of Lords that surrounded him. Even those that knew nothing about the rank he held could feel the power that Marcus exuded.

What was supposed to have been a quick stop for him, turned into an unplanned miniature goal(meeting). He spoke out to the surrounding crowd like a neighborhood political leader, with Peewee and Lil G standing directly by his side.

"I see y'all got the tip pumping like it 'posed to be, I like that," Marcus said to the 20 or more faces that stood in the circle. Every word Marcus spoke ignited the young Lords in his presence. "The only problem I got is that we had too many brothas either got shot or died on the strip in the past couple months..." Marcus paused and glanced around before continuing on, "What, y'all done kicked off a war wit'out me knowin'?" Marcus asked in a sardonic manner. Although Marcus wasn't raising his voice, his words were still tremendously felt. He woefully stated, "A couple weeks ago my lil brotha's best friend got murk'd out here jus' tryna' make some bread to feed his family." .

"He talkin' 'bout Randy, Jo..." A voice out the crowd muttered amongst the others standing next to him.

Marcus glanced around at the faces of his young mob and said, "So what'cha'll wanna do, go to war or get this paper? We can't do both at the same time."

One of the bolder shorties spoke up after a split second of silence. "I mean, we wanna get this paper Chief, but 'dem 'breeds off Kedzie been ridin' through here trippin' lately."

"Word got back to me that my people rode down on them niggas first at the liquor store on 19th," Marcus said, looking around for answers.

"Somebody had to pay for killin' Reesie," one of the heartless Shorties blurted out.

"So you took it upon yo'self to sanction a hit?" Marcus asked more vigorously, showing signs of his blood rising.

"Nah Chief," the youngster replied feeling the mood swing from the tone of Marcus's voice.

Turning to his left, Marcus asked, "Wee, you sent word?"

"Hell nawl!" Peewee assured.

Looking to the right of him he asked Lil G the same, "What about'chu Lil G, you sanctioned the hit?"

"Nope. Everybody knew to hold off 'til we got to the bottom of that shit," Lil G answered.

"Look here, the next time y'all wanna send out missions-n-shit without one of us givin' the word, you gon' have to see me!" Marcus expressed himself vehemently.

"From this day on, y'all ain't gon have to worry about a'mafucka comin' through here shootin' up shit! I'ma' make sure of that! Now if them niggas ride through here on bullshit any time after today, then y'all get ready to strap up, until then, get money! I know you lil niggas like to eat!" Marcus emphasized passionately.

"Hell yeah!" The group of young Lords roared back eagerly.

"A'ight then, Mighty!" Marcus hollered out after tapping his chest with the VL sign.

"Mighty!" The group chanted in response, throwing up the VL sign before scattering up and down 21st, resuming their hustling ways.

Before carrying on with Peewee and Lil G, Marcus stood there for a moment reflecting on how the new generation was changing right before his eyes. It seemed the late nineties and the new millennium was birthing a wilder, self-reliant breed of young hustlers. Back when Marcus and his clique first got into the organization, there were strict laws that had to be followed. The structure of the mob had definitely changed since the earlier years and Marcus was witnessing it firsthand.

While standing on the corner of Homan and 21st conversing with Lil G, Peewee, and a couple of others, a gold Crown Vic with only one detective inside drove slowly down the strip. In the middle of them talking, Marcus discreetly turned all of their attention toward the car that was passing by.

"Man, y'all saw who the fuck that was, right?!" Marcus asked astounded.

"Awe, man, that shit normal," Lil G said with a slight grin covering his face. "'Dem mothafuckas stay ridin' through here. They can't never find what they be lookin' for. Security stay on extra point."

"I did peep how he kind'a glanced over here and nodded his head, but I couldn't really see his face with that hat and them big ass glasses on," Peewee added, showing his normal insidious mug.

Looking as if a major thought was floating through his head, Marcus finally blurted out, "Man, that was mothafuckin' Chronin! I know that name ring a bell to y'all!"

"Damn, that's who 'dat was?!" Peewee replied with surprise. "I wonder what tha' fuck that was all about."

"Shhiiit, look around you," Lil G responded as if he was stating the obvious. Around them was nothing but crowds of fiends pacing back and forth anxiously looking for a fix. There were shorties on security, working packs, or guiding traffic down whichever block that had what the customers needed. Everything that created a super booming joint was in progress on the strip.

"Boa, I don't know what'chu done did to that last batch but that shit got these mothafuckas goin' crazy!" Lil G exclaimed, speaking to Marcus as they all paid attention to the chaotic scene going on around them.

Marcus couldn't deny the fact that he kept the dope that was prepared for the Lawndale community more raw and uncut to keep the potency high. Although the dope was still great in the other 'hoods that he governed through Rico, it was not great enough to cause complete havoc like it did on the 21st strip or 16th Street, areas that Marcus personally influenced.

As they continued to dissect the situation at hand, Marcus proceeded to say, "Well, one thing I do know, that ma'fucka jus' ain't joyridin' and decided to drive down one of the hottest strips on the Westside. When Chronin come through, its damn sho' a reason behind it."

Marcus's guys became accustomed to the police or slick boyz coming through sweatin' the blocks daily, but they surely weren't trying to see the type of heat that Chronin was capable of bringing down on them.

"So what we gon' do, Lord?" Peewee asked. "If it was up to me, I'a knock his ass off befo' he even start becomin' a problem." He stated coldheartedly before Marcus could respond. Marcus disregarded Peewee's suggestion instantly, knowing his homey was a menace and didn't give a fuck about killing the police. After getting shot up and almost dying twice, Peewee became even more dangerous and cared less about hurting anyone that got in their way.

As if Peewee said nothing, Lil G inferred, "I say we shut this ma'fucka down and relocate befo' we all be lookin' at indictments. You already kno' how that slimy mothafucka gets down."

"Why all of a sudden this ma'fucka wanna' pop up when I decide to come around..." a confused Marcus pondered while contemplating what needed to be done.

Any other time when the law was ready to intervene on any of Marcus's street operations, Big C would inform him before the heat fully came down. Marcus never thought about how he was getting his inside information. He figured since Big C was a longtime Chief it was inevitable for him to have crooked law enforcers on his payroll. Marcus was basically taking care of all Big C's business which allowed him to sit back and collect. So Marcus was entitled to the same advantages when it came down to the law, but without the hassle of dealing with them first hand. Marcus wondered to himself, "If Chronin up to some'nt why ain't I being informed?" Before jumping in his truck and peeling out Marcus eased his guy's nerves, "Aey look," Marcus spoke assertively, looking toward Lil G. "We jus' might have to close up for a minute. Give me a'couple days and I'a let'chu kno' some'nt, until then keep doin' what'chu do."

"Aight." Lil G replied with no questions asked.

Peewee hopped in the truck with Marcus as they chirped out. Lil G continued to patrol his strip as if nothing happened. He trusted Marcus's judgment and knew if something out of the ordinary was going on he would be urgently informed. Lil G was a real street dude and was well aware of the consequences that came along with the streets, so it was safe to say that he was willing to accept the good with the bad.

Chapter
29

Since the death of his best friend, Chris' basketball skills had taken a major slump. The unbelievable talents and tenacity he once displayed on the court now seemed average and not only his teammates but the entire basketball world that followed his illustrious high school career was sensing the change. The 30 and 40 point games turned into single digits. The dazzling moves that kept the crowd in awe had come to a complete halt. Chris was merely going through the motions and did just enough to get his team to the playoffs. The Warriors went from being number one ranked in the city to third due to Chris' downgraded performances.

It was the last game of the season and the Bulldogs were playing a team that had no chance of making the playoffs. The Warriors were leading the game by a large margin and Chris spent majority of the second half on the bench. During blowout games, the scene on the bench usually was a bunch of teenagers enjoying themselves and joking around with one another and Randy was the cornerstone. That joy amongst the team was long gone. The entire team mourned over the loss of their fellow teammate but Chris took it to heart. Seeing one of his best friends buried six feet under and his grandmother being in an unstable medical condition was really taking a toll on Chris's psyche and it showed in his everyday actions.

A few of his closest teammates had made countless attempts to brighten Chris's spirits. They made another heartfelt attempt, knowing if they had any chance of winning a second city and state championship they were going to need his undivided focus.

Chris was sitting at the end of the bench in silence with a large towel covering his head when Antwone, Dante, and a few others made it their business to get their homey's attention.

While laughing at a joke cracked by one of the players that had everyone in disarray, Dante looked to his side and saw that Chris hadn't budged.

"Chris, wassup man," Dante blurted out, bumping shoulders with Chris causing him to shift to the side, which broke him out of his trance. "You a'ight?"

"I ain't been feelin' too good." Chris simply replied with his attention swaying back into a daydream.

"You ain't been feelin' too good for the past month now," Dante stated humorously. "Maybe we need to rush you to a hospital."

"Naw, I'm cool." Chris rejected his friends mocking suggestion with all seriousness.

"Look Chris, this me you talkin' to, Jo. I kno' when some'nt bothering you," Dante said, gaining everyone's attention that sat around them. "I'm sayin', you don't think we all fucked up behind what happened to Randy? That was my mothafuckin' nigga too, no matter how much we stayed into it..." He stated in an emotional manner. "I kno' you feel responsible for how it went down but you can't go the rest of yo' life blaming ya'self for what God had already planned. When it's our time to check up outta' here, ain't nuttin' we could do about it. I'm sure Randy wouldn't want us to be around here wit' sad faces anyway. You feel me." Dante finished his statement sounding more like a motivational speaker than a high school ball player.

"Yeah, I feel you, my nigga." Chris solemnly said forcing himself to smile. He couldn't deny feeling better after a rare wholehearted speech from his friend.

"Now that we got that out the way, my nigga, you have been playin' like some straight garbage lately!" Antwone blatantly intervened while sitting on the other side of Chris, causing the others to burst out in laughter.

Realizing how reckless Antwone's mouth could get at times, Chris simply shrugged at his outburst

174

before stating, "I'on kno', I guess I jus' ain't been feeling this shit lately."

"Well I kno' one thing, the playoffs start next week and we gon' need you to start killin'," Antwone said.

"And not only that," Randy began to say. "You got all them critics out there doubting ya' skillz, writing all 'dat bullshit about'chu in the paper. You don't want these scouts to start thinking they been making a mistake on ya' game all these years. You gotta ball out!"

"Or else we gon' be watchin' yo ass play up at Malcolm X Junior College!" Antwone blurted out, causing everyone to laugh again as Chris reacted by playfully attacking his friend. He couldn't help but loosen up after what had been said.

Their mission was complete. Chris seemed to be out of his depressed mode and was ready to get the ball rolling again. A majority of the Division I schools had been following Chris' career since his 8th grade year. He definitely didn't want his dreams of playing for a Division I college and possibly going on to the pros to go down the drain.

Peewee walked towards a deli market on 13th and Kedzie that was owned by Arab's, but run by the Newbreeds or 'Breeds. He was accompanied by a couple of his young soldiers. They were on their way to pay the 'Breeds' 'hood general a visit. Marcus and the Lieutenant of the Newbreed mob set up a meeting to put an end to the war that had caused so many unnecessary deaths on both sets.

"I hate meetin' up wit' these weak ass niggas," Peewee grumbled to the three Lords that accompanied him as they briskly stomped their way inside the store.

The young Arabian behind the counter was awaiting their arrival. Just as they walked in, he exited to the back of the store and within seconds he reemerged, escorting Peewee and the others to a backroom that looked more like a kitchenette. The young Arabian tried to frisk Peewee and the Lords but a voice stopped him before there was any.

"Aey, Q, that ain't necessary, announced Alonzo, the young lieutenant for the 'Breeds. "They all good.".

Alonzo was young and wild and he had a crew of 'Breeds that were just as wild in the section he governed. Peewee and Alonzo knew each other well from years of being around nearby neighborhoods. Their sets were so close they practically grew up around each other and knew a lot about both generations. Alonzo came into the picture with the younger generation and had some respect for Peewee and the Lords off 21st. He knew Peewee was a vicious killer and had one of the richest street guys on the West Side, Marcus, by his side. Still, Alonzo was a loose cannon and would stir up strife to get his point across, even when his chances of winning a war were slim to none.

With a couple of guys standing in the back background, Alonzo walked up and greeted Peewee cordially.

"Wee, wassup wit'chu baby." He extended his hand. Peewee didn't accept the welcoming hand and both crews wore matching mean mugs.

"Aey, man, you niggas kno' how the fuck I get down. Why y'all actin' like y'all want these problems?" Peewee exclaimed in an ominous manner despite being on dangerous grounds.

"Hol, hol, hol, we 'posed to be here for a peace treaty, not warfare," the young, clever lieutenant said. "Remember, we ain't the ones who kicked this shit off. My lil cousin was one of them three that died when y'all decide to shoot up the liquor sto'. You think I 'posed to sit back and jus' let that shit ride!

"...Y'all niggas killed Reesie!" One of the young Lords shouted out, causing a slight commotion to rise up from both sides.

"We 'bout money, we ain't have no reason to be fuckin' wit'cha'll. It's some shit goin' on within y'all own circle."

"Aey, chill out!" Peewee looked to his side and settled his guys down. "The only reason I ain't ova' here terrorizing you mothafuckas every chance I—"

"Hol'on potna', we ain't worried 'bout'chu terrorizin' shit over here!" After cutting Peewee short of his statement, Alonzo took a couple steps back and the sounds of guns clacking filled the room. In an instant, 'Breeds came from everywhere with semi-automatics. The Lords drew down their pistols, but it was obvious that they were outnumbered and had no chance of walking out of there alive.

During the standoff, Alonzo glanced around and saw he had a clear advantage and sardonically recited a line from the move The Mack, "Now we can handle this like gentlemen or we can get on some gansta' shit, your choice."

Peewee wasn't fazed by the tight situation. He stared Alonzo square in the eye and said, "Them gunz y'all got pointin' don't mean shit. You fuckin' wit'a nigga 'dats ready to die," he fearlessly said. "Now I advise you to keep them lil niggas in check befo' I do."

Walking from the back of the deli, Peewee looked around and lowly proclaimed, "Lil scary mothafuckas ain't gon' kill shit or let nuttin' die..."

Alonzo and his crew knew that Peewee meant every word. After being shot nine times and surviving, Peewee's veins pumped ice water and dying was the least of his worries. Although Alonzo showed no remorse amongst his guys as he watched Peewee and the Lords leave, in the back of his mind he wondered about the move that he had just made. Not only did he have to worry about Peewee coming back for him but he also had to think about the bosses of his organization coming down on him. The bold move was not authorized and both mobs were striving to prevent an unnecessary war. This was another sign of the new millennium street guys being rebellious and wild with no conscience. Obeying rules and commands was slowly leaving their realm of thinking. They just didn't give a fuck about nothing or nobody!

Rico's reign as a five star universal elite for the IVL's was at an all-time high. The entire West Side knew his name and the areas he controlled. The streets honored his position with the mob but it was mostly out of fear. Under the discreet guidance of Smitty, he was even able to conquer land in the Wild Hunits. Rico was getting more money than he had ever touched in his life.

Rico drove through different blocks off Cicero in his cherry red, cream interior 2000 Lexus coupe sitting on 22 inch factory chrome with one of his personal goons assisting him. Rico's time wasn't required out South as much after laying the law down and personally demonstrating treacherous acts towards those that didn't comply. After appointing different positions to certain honorable Lords from the area, everything began running routinely.

Rico was enjoying all the energetic attention from all the bystanders. As he accelerated down one of the side blocks off Cicero, a phone call came through. Glancing down at his cell, Rico recognized the number and quickly answered.

"Hello."

"How you doin' young brotha'?" The masculine voice on the other end responded.

"Every thang good, I really cain't complain. How about'cha self?" Rico asked with humility in his tone while speaking to his long time commander in Chief, Smitty. Whenever these two conversed, they always spoke in code, never revealing names or any mob affiliations. Their points were always sent across clearly. Although Smitty never made direct calls from the penitentiary, they never took any chances knowing it was a definite possibility that the Feds could be listening at any given time.

"I'm jus' maintaining, taking it one day at a time."

"Yeah...don't trip, them next five years gon' fly pass befo' you know it," Rico said, sending encouraging words as he referred to the duration of Smitty's bid.

"So, how that wicked world out there been treatin' you?"

"Well, you kno', I'ma good guy, I make the world like me." Rico replied in a slick manner followed by a laugh.

"How about the household? You been takin' care of home base?" Smitty firmly asked.

"Awe yeah, every thang copasetic. Sometimes the wife be tryna act up but once I straighten her out, we become tight again." Rico said, referring to the West Side and the occasional mishaps that go on.

"That's always good to hear. Gotta keep the family straight," Smitty said. "I been tryna' get in touch wit'cha' big brotha'. He seems to be the hardest person in the world to get up wit'. Every time I reach out, I get no response." Smitty stated, making references to Marcus.

"The only time I really see 'em is when we go to the house for Sunday dinner and that's once a month," Rico responded, admitting to the fact that he only saw Marcus when it was time to re-up and collect money.

"Ever since he started that new job, he's been more and more out of sight."

"Well, you kno', I ain't got no problem with him not being seen as much, that's a good thang," Smitty said. "I did talk to him a while back. I gave him a heads up about a situation. I sent out a kite and informed him on a lingering disease that's likely gon' spread and affect all of us. He was supposed to be that cure..."

Rico pulled over on a side block as his attention span grew profoundly.

"...After I sent word letting him kno' the disease was close to home, he haven't made himself available since. His disregard to a direct order isn't sitting too well with the community around me," Smitty said, sounding like an intelligent street professor in lecture mode as he gave Rico an ear full.

182

"We're startin' to believe that he's become a part of the epidemic instead of part of the solution."

"Pardon the body," Rico interrupted honorably. "Why you ain't send me to detect the disease? You kno' I help heal people well."

"This medical situation is critical and it was to be dealt with accordingly," Smitty firmly claimed, knowing that an attempted assassination on Big C had to be planned to perfection without anyone suspecting it to be an inside job. Smitty went on to say, "...but we as a community in here do need you to send a small, discreet message to your big brotha'. Nuttin' too major, jus' enough for him to understand he still can be reached."

Rico sat there in complete awe of the information that he'd just received. He couldn't believe he had been elected to bring such torment upon someone of such magnitude. Rico tried to read between the lines as Smitty spoke. He couldn't pinpoint who Smitty was insinuating to be the disease carrier, but he knew it could be detrimental to the mob as a whole.

Rico would do anything for Smitty and the VL Nation, even if it meant bringing pain upon a high official to get their attention. After staring into space with devilish thoughts racing through his mind, Rico responded, "Yeah, I got'chu'. I think I got jus' the thing in mind."

"Okay...You be careful out there."

"All the time. I'a get wit'chu later."

183

"Peace," Smitty said as they both disconnected from each other.

Once ending the call, Rico continued on his journey riding through different 'hoods while contemplating his next mission.

31

Marcus pulled up in the rear parking lot of Conservative Formal Men's Wear clothing store located in the Ashland business district. The store was owned by an Italian with Big C as a silent partner. Marcus was on the way to deliver his monthly package to Big C, which was roughly a hundred thousand. On this particular day Marcus had Marlin alongside him. It was unusual for Marlin to be off his post, but whenever Marcus called, he moved with no questions asked. Marlin had the blocks off Cermak on smash and operating smoothly. He always made sure Marcus got what he needed and by him operating the 'dro through the land, he was getting a lot of cash on his own terms. Out of Marcus's five childhood friends, Marlin was progressing the most in the money department. Mainly because he stayed in the field and kept his eyes and ears open to other hustling opportunities instead of waiting on Marcus to make a way all the time. Even though Marlin didn't have rank in the mob, he felt as long as Marcus sat in the highest seat he was entitled to do whatever he wanted on the blocks in the neighborhood that they all grew up in. As long as he didn't disrespect the mob in anyway, Marcus had no problem with him making other moves. In fact, Marcus respected his mindset and was willing to invest in any business moves Marlin brought to his attention.

Needless to say, when these two were together they smoked liked a chimney. With Marlin supplying the 'dro, they had more than their share of blunts to smoke. Marlin had been a true weed smoker since their younger days. Now that he had his hands on a better grade of weed, he stayed higher than life. These days Marcus smoked everyday just to keep his sanity. The position that he held in the mob caused the type of stress that would drive a normal person crazy.

Marcus surveyed the parking lot before getting out of his truck. He noticed a couple of Benz's parked directly next to the Big C's recently purchased, antique Rolls Royce that was banana peel yellow with a dark brown leather top. The Rolls was an 80's model and Big C was the first and only person to ever expose a foreign car of that magnitude to the 'hood.

With Marlin toting the Fendi duffle bag, they both walked towards the three level building. Marcus pressed the intercom and announced his name. A few seconds passed before the thick, metal door cracked open. A tall, muscular white guy, obviously of Italian descent, welcomed them. As they walked through the door, they saw a staircase and a freight elevator that went up only two floors. Instead of going up another level, they headed through a door on the ground level. The door led them to the back of the clothing store where the dressing room and tailor shop was located. After passing through the dressing room, they entered the main area. The store was exquisite, with two levels of expensive formal wear and shoes for men. There were glass mirrors, leather sofas, and oak hardwood floors throughout. Marcus and Marlin were standing there awestruck when Big C walked up to them with his business partner alongside him.

"There he is. The man of the city!" Big C raved about Marcus. "Paulie, my godson, Marcus. Marcus, this my business partner Paulie," he smiled and casually put his arm around Paulie's neck and continued "...the genius behind putting this illustrious establishment together."

"Marcus, a pleasure, guy. Trust me, I heard a lot of great things about you," Paulie said with a delighted grin as they shook hands.

Paulie looked to be in his early forties. His skin tone was deathly pale and he had big, dark bags underneath his eyes. You could tell that he hardly got enough sleep. He was sharply dressed in a metallic-grey tailored double breasted suit. His jet black hair was slicked back and he wore rings on both hands and a Cartier watch. It was apparent that this guy kept himself groomed to perfection. Despite Marcus and Marlin stepping inside the clothing store reeking of marijuana, the loud scent of Paulie's expensive fragrance polluted the air.

After Marcus and Paulie exchanged a few acknowledging words, Big C turned his attention towards Marlin and greeted him cynically. "Whudd up slick," he addressed Marlin while staring him down. Big C was familiar with Marlin, but he was more accustomed to seeing Peewee, Lil G, or J.R. beside Marcus during business transactions. "I hope you got them eyes open while y'all ridin' them streets," Big C pointedly directed his comment to Marlin. "We can't afford no more slip ups."

It was clear as day that Marcus and Marlin were under the influence from their feel good facial expressions. Big C disliked Marcus's smoking habits, but he showed even more displeasure when his guys, who was supposed to have is back, was in worse condition. Marlin had no response, he knew Big C was referring to the assassination attempt against Marcus a while back. Big C smoked cigarettes and was an occasional drinker, but he never experimented with any other drug. All of Marcus's guys were heavy smokers, but for the most part, they stayed on their square.

Glancing down at the duffle bag that Marlin held, Big C stated, "I assume that's for me?" After getting a slight nod of approval from Marcus, Marlin handed over the Fendi bag. "I'll get to that later," Big

188

C said as he tossed the bag full of neatly stacked large bills to the side as if it wasn't important. "Paulie, let's hook my boys up with some custom made linen suits, on the house."

"No problem," Paulie said as he unraveled the tape measure that was hanging around his neck. "Let me size you gentlemen up and get you in some of the finest linen you'll ever put on your body." Paulie said in a cocky manner.

The offer sounded all good to Marlin, but Marcus had other issues on his mind.

"Paulie, go 'head and size my man up while I holla at C," Marcus said as he pulled Big C to the side. A concerned expression formed on Big C's mug as while he and Marcus headed towards the back of the store.

"What's goin' on? You a'ight?" Big C curiously asked while putting an arm around Marcus neck.

"Naw, not really," Marcus said, cutting right to the chase. "The other day I jus' happened to be standing out on 21st and that slime ass Chronin rode through the strip. He kind'a looked my way and threw a nod." Big C's body language suddenly changed. He began showing some uneasiness once he heard the name of the most ferocious detective that side of town had seen.

"You ain't heard nuttin' 'bout 'dem people making a move my way, have you?" Marcus asked, his tone sounding more agitated than honorable.

Big C sensed the vibe change and attempted to reclaim comfort between him and Marcus.

"Now you kno' damn well if I heard some'nt you would've been the first person I came to holla at. Ain't that's how it's always been?"

"Yeah..." Marcus raised both eyebrows and agreed undeniably.

"So, what makes you think the shit'll change up now?" Big C questioned.

"I'on kno' C. It jus' didn't look right."

"Well if it didn't look right, you need to shut them joints down and let me check up on some. Make sure not another crumb is sold on 21st until I tell you otherwise. Chronin is one mothafucka we don't wanna' fuck wit'." Big C assured, showing a level of respect for the Colombo look-a-like.

Although Marcus was a heavy weed smoker, he was still considered a thinker and moved around unpredictably. Marcus seemed to contemplate situations much deeper after smoking.

Big C thought his job of easing Marcus nerves was complete so he turned his attention back to the clothes.

"Don't let that shit worry you; you kno' I gotcha' back baby," he stated. "Now gone out there and finish getting fitted up so you can getcha' grown man on." He laughed, but didn't get the same response out of Marcus.

"You kno' what? I'ma have to take a rain check today." Marcus said.

"You sure...?"

"Yeah, I gotta run," Marcus said while looking down at his multi-colored diamond bezel wristwatch from Jacob the Jeweler. "I 'posed to met up wit' this nigga fifteen minutes ago. I'on wanna keep 'em waitin' too long."

"Okay, I'on wanna stop you from handlin' ya' bin'nis. Jus' make sho' you come back and grab some of this exclusive shit!" Big C exclaimed.

"I'a most definitely be back," Marcus replied as they shook up and gave each other shoulder daps. "You kno' this my style anyway."

Marcus couldn't deny that the clothing was exclusive and pretty expensive, but his mind had shifted to things more important than clothes.

Marlin was able to get a couple linen short outfits with the casual shoes to match before being signaled by Marcus. Right before making their exit Big C hollered out, "Aye, Marcus," they both turned to look back. "Tell that ole man of yours to get at me befo' I have to put out an APB on his ass. It ain't like him to go a whole week without hol'lin at me." He stated half-jokingly with a sense of suspense.

"I'a make sho' I get on'em fa' you, C." Marcus matched his humor before heading toward the door.

"A'ight, y'all be careful out there. And make sure you remember what I told you, not another crumb!" He forcefully reminded.

"I got'chu," Marcus assured him as they exited the building.

Since doing he began doing business with Big C, this the first time Marcus ever left his presence not feeling the same genuineness that he normally felt when they met with each other.

Damn...Maybe Smitty was right about dude...
Marcus felt a sense of paranoia as he maneuvered
out the parking space. I'on care what Steve say, I
might have to check up on that shit. He continued
his reckless thinking while Marlin flamed up a ready
rolled Swisher Sweet.   Marcus accelerated down
Ashland and headed back toward the neighborhood.

32

After undergoing several tests and being misdiagnosed a couple of times, Sylvia took it upon herself to have her mother seen by specialists at the University of Illinois-Chicago Medical Center. After running advanced testing, the doctors discovered the problem causing Grandma Emma's illness. Before revealing any information, the doctor insisted that the immediate family be present.

On a beautiful, lazy Sunday afternoon, Sylvia called the Williams family up to the hospital. All of Grandma Emma's children and her older grandchildren were all gathered around her hospital bed waiting for the doctor to arrive; not even Grandma Emma knew what the results from the test were. When the casually dressed, extremely short Asian woman stepped inside the room she witnessed the family in good spirits, consoling their queen, hoping for the best.

"Hello everyone," the doctor entered with charts in hand, speaking joyfully. "My name is

Doctor Huang." Everyone spoke back with expressions of optimism covering their faces. The doctor setup charts on a display board and began stating facts.

"I requested the family to be present to provide a well needed moral support system for Mrs. Williams," she spoke out sincerely.

"Now, my staff and I have completed several advanced tests so that we could single out the problem.

The Doctor directed everyone's attention toward the charts in front of them before explaining what the diagrams meant.

"Because Mrs. Williams had such an intense cough, my team of doctors focused more on her heart and lungs. Her heart is perfectly fine. When it was time to examine the condition of her lungs we expected some sort of damage because she has been a chain smoker for so many years. In most cases, it's usually fluids that have accumulated around the lungs that cause the type of symptoms that she has shown." Dr. Huang paused before making a statement in regards to the three different photos of lung conditions posted in front of her. "However in Mrs. Williams' case, we found malignant tumors throughout her lungs."

Since everyone was standing around looking dumbfounded at the medical jargon that the doctor was using, Sylvia asked for clarification.

"So, is there any way that these tumors could be treated or possibly cleared away?"

"Only if detected in its earlier stages," Dr. Huang explained. She pointed to the photo that most resembled Grandma Emma's lung condition. "As you can see, these photos are different phases the lungs go through when a person suffers from this condition. Unfortunately Mrs. Williams wasn't admitted soon enough for us to catch the problem in time."

"Doctor Huang, what are you indicating?" Sylvia timidly asked with the rest of the family sitting on pins and needles feeling their hopes of any good news becoming slim to none.

Dr. Huang paused before speaking. She did not like revealing bad news to families.

"I'm afraid Mrs. Williams has been diagnosed with stage three lung cancer. At this stage there's very little we can do to keep the cancer from spreading."

Once the word cancer was mentioned, it deflated air out of everyone in the room and caused all faces to drop. Some family members were so emotional that they rushed out of the room with their hands covering their faces to keep from showing their tears. Marcus, Chris, and Sylvia all stood the closest to Grandma Emma when they heard the news. They all tried hard to be strong and keep straight faces, but Sylvia seemed to have the most strength out of them all. She softly caressed her mother's face while whispering encouraging words to assure her everything was going to be alright.

With tears flowing down her smooth precious cheeks, Grandma Emma's facial expression showed sorrow and her soul seemed dispirited. Out of all the people standing around her, she glanced up at Marcus with an aching expression as if she was looking to him for answers. Marcus couldn't bear the painful feeling any longer as tears began flowing down his face like a running faucet. All the money in the world couldn't recompense not having his grandmother. He would give up everything in the world to switch places with the queen of his life.

Out of nowhere Grandma Emma bluntly asked, "Doctor, how long do I have to live?" Everyone looked over at her with discontent. The family still had hope and dreaded to hear any more bad news. Dr. Huang proceeded to give different options that would help treat the cancer.

"We do offer chemotherapy and radiology sessions to help slow the growth of the tumors and prevent them from breaking down other organs. The downside to those treatments are the side effects. The pain could be extremely severe. However, without these treatments, Mrs. William's condition has no chance of improving."

"What are some of the side effectsthat we can expect?" Sylvia cautiously asked.

"Extreme body aches, loss of appetite, and she may eventually experience some hair loss. In spite of those side effects, we do have treatments to compensate for everything she'll be lacking. To ease the pain, we'll prescribe morphine, that way she'll be able to rest without feeling any pain." The doctor spoke in a soothing tone, trying everything in her soul to comfort the grieving family. "Now, we have a team of specialists who only treat cancer and I can assure you all that we'll work to the best of our ability to keep Mrs. Williams with us. But most importantly she needs spiritual and emotional support from her family to have any chance at beating this. The average life expectancy for someone with stage three cancer is usually around three months."

Doctor Huang's statement ripped the family's hearts out. Everyone stood around with long faces and began mourning as if Grandma Emma had already died. The family was speechless as the doctor left the room. Sylvia spoke up and forcibly lashed out at all the sad faces around her.

"Look, this is exactly what Momma doesn't need! We all have to go to God and ask Him for the strength to get us through this! The good Lord hasn't failed us in all these years and I don't think He'll start now!"

Sylvia's motivational speech brought tears, but at the same time, it uplifted everyone, if only for a moment . In all actuality, the family didn't know where to begin to show the type of support their mother needed. In defiance of the news, Marcus stood there staring in space with a look of determination covering his face. He couldn't watch his grandmother suffer. At that very moment, he

197

decided to help her fight the endless battle and prove the doctor's three-month prediction wrong.

The stage was set at the United Center. There were over 10,000 fans in attendance to witness the public school city championship game between two West Side schools, the Westinghouse Warriors and the Whitney Young Cougars. Clearly, the crowd was there to see the top point guard in the city, Chris. Westinghouse ranked third in the Red West conference while the number one ranked Whitney Young had only one loss all season.

Chris was extremely focused during warm-ups. It looked as though he had a chip on his shoulder. The entire team had on some type of accessory in remembrance of their teammate, but Chris took it to another level. He switched his jersey number from 11 to 25 in honor of his deceased teammate and best friend, Randy.

Most of the people in the crowd were normal high school basketball fans. In addition to the regulars, there were a few well-known street figures that usually never showed up to such public events.

In the pre-game layup line, Chris' teammates kept interrupting his one-track mind by pointing out different faces in the crowd. Jogging to the back of the line one of his teammates excitedly hollered out, "Damn Jo, you kno' this game gotta be the talk of the city if Rico showed up!" He then pointed toward the section where Rico and his crew were stationed. Chris scanned around and caught a glimpse of a few cold stares come his way from that particular section, but thought nothing of it. Since he was a high school phenom, he had experienced that often.

"If Rico in the building I kno' yo' brotha' gotta be around here somewhere!" His teammate exclaimed, showing obvious signs of being infatuated by 'hood stars.

"Naw man, since we found out about my Gran'ma that nigga ain't lef' her bed side," Chris said in the midst of receiving a pass and racing towards the basket to put up a fancy finger roll.

Like everybody else, Chris knew all about Rico. Even though Marcus and Rico were the top heads for the same mob, Chris didn't feel the need to acknowledge him. Chris never met Rico before. He only had a personal relationship with Marcus's long time crew and other leaders from the Holy City area.

"There he go. Our star player. The only player we came to see." Rico spoke to his crew of Lords from out South while studying Chris's every move.

"Aw yea, that's shorty who always be in the paper. He definitely goin' places." One of the Lords said, seeming to be the only basketball literate person out of the group. Everyone else's minds were on the mission at hand. Rico stood in complete silence with his all black, Buck Fifty snakeskin brim cap tilted to the left. Rico's focus stayed directly on Chris as he ignored all the wandering eyes that came from every street nigga and female gold digger that crossed his path.

From the tip-off, Chris came out dominating. He scored the Bulldogs first three baskets in less than a minute by attacking the basket with fierceness. The Bulldogs team defense was tenacious. They put the clamps down on Whitney Young's best players and caused early turnovers that resulted in fast break points. Halfway through the first quarter, Chris took a pass at the top of the three-point arc, drove into the thick of the defense, and lofted up a rainbow floater, hitting nothing but net! Less than a minute later, he stepped into a contested three point shot and made it. On the very next possession, Chris took his defender off the dribble on the high left side, making his way awkwardly to the baseline, putting up an off balance jumper with two defenders in his face. His expression looked as though he knew it was going in, and it did!

Chris, who had been struggling halfway through the season, was now playing out of his mind. His lightning speed allowed him to blow past the defense effortlessly. By the end of the first half, Chris had only missed two shots from the three-point line, hit all five of his free throw attempts, and scored 30 points, tying his own school record for most points scored in a half. Although Marcus and Sylvia were missing in action, Steve managed to show up and witness the classical performance that his son was putting on. However, despite Chris' dominance his team went into half time with only a slim lead.

During the break, Chris kept to himself with his mind deadlocked on the game. It was unusual for him not to celebrate with his teammates after putting on such a spectacular showcase, but his teammates and the coaching staff respected his space. They were well aware of the recent hardships he was dealing with. Besides, Chris was playing the best game they had ever seen out of him throughout his years at Westinghouse.

As soon as the whistle blew to start the second half, Chris immediately resumed playing with the same intensity. He came out making a statement by hitting his first five shots. Two of them were three point field goals. The Cougars fought to keep the score respectable despite having no answer for Chris. They had a versatile 6'7" power forward named Jimmy Brooks that very well kept them in the game. He was just as star-studded as Chris was and he was definitely a Division I prospect. All season long sports anchors labeled him as a Kevin Garnett type of player because of his size and strength. Some thought he was capable of going from high school directly to the NBA. The entire season Jimmy destroyed every player that stood in his way.

By the end of the third quarter, Chris and Jimmy were well above their season averages. Jimmy 25 points, 12 rebounds, and a couple of blocks. He had averaged a double-double throughout the entire season. Chris on the other hand averaged 28 points, eight assist, and three steals, but this championship game he had 45 points through three quarters and he wasn't showing any signs of letting up!

Going into the fourth quarter, the Bulldogs were leading by seven. The Cougars came out with different defensive schemes hoping to slow down Chris, but it was to no avail. Chris adjusted to the frequent double teams by playing off the ball. When he had no space to maneuver, he found his open teammates with no problem, racking up on assists. Midway through the fourth quarter, Chris had already topped his career high with fifty points and the crowd was ecstatic! The breakout game everyone was waiting for was happening right before their eyes. Out of all Chris' outstanding performances, this championship game was by far turning out to be his best.

In the midst of a late fourth quarter rally, Jimmy threw down a monstrous two-hand jam that brought the crowd to their feet! The Cougars came within two baskets with a little under four minutes left in the game. Jimmy had just broken the 30-point mark and his team was showing signs of being rejuvenated. The Cougars were a resilient, championship caliber team and was accustomed to making late game comebacks. While their minds were set on making a miraculous comeback after being down the entire game, Chris was steadily piling up on his point total, surging to become the highest scoring point guard ever in a city's championship game.

With 1:26, left to play Chris was on his 58th point and the Bulldogs had the possession. Coming off two back door screens, Chris was able to shake loose of his defender and receive a pass well beyond the three-point arc. Instead of the two defenders running toward him to get the ball out of his hands, he experienced an unusual switch up. Jimmy's 6'7" wiry frame stood firmly in front of Chris in a lock down defensive stance, forcefully dismissing the oncoming double team. The seconds were ticking off the clock. Chris began to make his move. He put on a series of deliberate, zigzagging spin moves that got him 10 feet from the basket before knocking down a difficult step back, a one-footed fall away that could not have been better defended. The Cougars immediately called a timeout after that display from Chris.

The basket put the Warriors back up by four with a little over a minute left and it gave Chris an unprecedented 60 points! As they came out of the timeout, it was obvious the play was drawn up for their best player. After forcing a pass to Jimmy, he attacked the rim and drew a foul. Since he wasn't a good free throw shooter, it was shocking that he nailed them both. It was back to a two-point game.

The Cougars were dedicated to denying Chris the ball after he made the free throw and this time they were successful and caused a collapse in the Bulldogs offense. The Cougars recovered the turnover and ran a set play that got them a good look from the perimeter. After they made a field goal to even the score, they quickly went to a full court press. Chris got to the ball and was fouled immediately. He went to the foul line for two shots with 20 seconds left on the game clock. Chris was the Bulldog's best free throw shooter. He stepped up and knocked the first shot down as if there was no pressure. He took a couple of breaths, poised himself, and shot the second free throw. Unfortunately, it rimmed out. The Cougars attacked the offensive boards, giving themselves one last chance at victory. Having no timeouts left, the Cougars point guard was forced to take it coast to coast. Jimmy Brooks received the ball 20 feet away from the basket, way out of his comfort zone, and posted up a tough, contested fade away with the time running out. The shot looked to be on line, but failed to fall through as it came off the back rim. After a brief scramble for the rebound time expired and the Westinghouse Warriors were declared the city champions for the third straight year!

Overwhelmed with joy, Chris stood at center court and flipped his jersey over his face. Seconds later, he was bombarded by his team and fans. His teammates all piled up on each other in celebration turning the court into complete mayhem! All the sport reporters were anxious to get an interview with the superstar. When they saw a chance to pull Chris away from all the commotion, they proceeded to tug at him.

"Christopher! Christopher!" The CLTV sports anchor hysterically called his name in hopes of getting his attention. Chris was still distracted by the surrounding excitement. Before taking the interview, he insisted on finding his Pops. Once that was accomplished, he proceeded with the interview with Steve standing beside him.

With a celebration soaring all around them and the cameras was rolling. the sportscaster began his questioning.

"Mark Weigel, broadcasting live from the United Center, I'm standing here with the Westinghouse Bulldogs standout, Christopher Williams." After looking into the camera, he then turned to face Chris. "Christopher tell us, how in the world were you able to come out and put on such a remarkable game on such a huge stage after struggling throughout the second half of the season?"

Standing there with his dad's arm around his neck and people constantly walking pass congratulating him, Chris managed to say, "This year has been pretty tough for me. We lost a teammate, Randy Robinson, who was also my best friend. My grandmother, the love of my life, was recently diagnosed with cancer. It's jus' been a lot goin' on in my life and I wanted to come out and dedicate this game to them." Chris humbly answered while still slightly winded.

"So what's the reason behind the sudden number change?"

"Yeah," Chris said as he grabbed hold of his jersey and looked dead into the camera. "Rest in peace Randy! This one for you, boy!"

"So what about the extraordinary 61 points you scored? Was there any significance behind your point total?"

"When I seen it was reachable that's when I remembered my grandmother's age and began shooting for 61," Chris looked into the camera and said, "I love you Granny! We gon' make it through this!" Chris became slightly choked up after his statement.

"On behalf of CLTV we send our best wishes to your grandmother and again, congratulations on your third city championship! We look forward to seeing you guys down in Peoria to compete for the state championship..." The sportscaster ended his interview after seeing Chris' eagerness to continue his celebration with the rest of the team.

After the trophy ceremony at center court, the team resumed its celebration in the locker room. The partying was far from over for most of the team as everyone began making plans for an after party. In the middle of discussing plans, Chris made a statement that startled his teammates.

"Aey y'all, I'ma chill wit' my girl tonight and get ready for the trip. I ain't really in no partying mood."

"You mean to tell me you ain't gon' kick it wit' the fellas after that show you jus' put on?" Dante asked in disbelief.

"Nawl, not tonight, I'a catch up witcha'll tomorrow at the team meeting." Chris dapped his teammates up in a distressing manner. Even though he had just experienced the game of his life, the grief remained. The team fully understood what Chris was going through and respected his wishes, but that definitely didn't deter their plans.

When Chris left the locker room, he was met by his father and a few lingering reporters. As the reporters rapidly sputtered out different questions concerning the game, Chris continued his course towards his father. Departing the stadium doors onto the parking lot, Chris and Steve both were giving their exciting recap on Chris's "game of the century."

"Where the rest of the guys? I kno' damn well y'all boyz 'bout to get into some'nt!" Steve joked.

"Not tonight Pops. I made plans wit' one of my lady friends." Chris smiled on the sly, referring to sexual activities. Chris and his father had an open relationship when it came to the ladies. Steve didn't mind Chris seeing different females as long as it didn't interfere with the more important things in his young life.

208

"Look at'choo, ditching ya' potna's for a piece of ass?! What type of friend are you?" Steve lashed out sarcastically.

Chris humbly laughed out loud at Steve's humor as he attempted to say, "...Naw man, it ain't like 'dat...'"

"You ain't gotta explain, son. Hell, if it was me I'a prob'le do the same thang." They both shared a laugh and gave each other five. Before leaving his son's presence, Steve made a few fatherly demands. "Aey, whateva' you get into tonight, don't let it take away from your focus. You still got some unfinished business to handle on that court."

"I got'chu Pops,"

"And make sho' you getcha' ass up there to that hospital in the morning."

They embraced each other once again with a manly hug before walking off. Chris's car was parked a few feet from where they stood while Steve had to walk a block away to get to his car. Chris got into his Regal and maneuvered out of the lot onto a dark side street that had few cars parked along the curb. He noticed headlights appear in his rearview mirror that he hadn't seen when he first pulled out the lot. Chris watched the lights in the mirror until he reached Madison Avenue, a busier street, then lost them in the traffic.

The next morning at UIC Medical Center, Marcus sat quietly beside his grandmother while she slept peacefully. The only sound coming from the room were the constant drops of IV fluids and the beeps from her heart monitor. Grandma Emma was highly sedated with morphine, which allowed her to rest without feeling any excruciating pain. Marcus was so in tune with watching his grandmother sleep he didn't hear the nurse enter the room.

"Excuse me, sir," the nurse softly called out from behind, snapping Marcus out of a deep trance. "I'm so sorry to disturb you, but it's time for Mrs. Williams' daily treatment." Marcus carefully pecked his grandmother's cheek before whispering in her ear, "Everything gon' be okay Momma, I promise. Imma be here every step of the way, you hear me. I love you." He spoke in hopes for a response. Marcus hesitated to leave the room as the doctors began to administer her treatment.

As Marcus rode the elevator down to the ground floor, the exhaustion from not getting enough sleep started to take hold of him. All he could think about was getting some rest then making his way back up to the hospital where he'd been spending most of his days and nights. Marcus's availability to the streets was cut short after finding out about his grandmother's illness. The moment he stepped out of the hospital doors and powered on his phone, it immediately alerted him that the voice mail was full. Marcus hadn't had his phone on for a whole minute before an incoming call came through. He was reluctant to answer because he was not in a good mood, but after noticing the number calling was from Steve he made an exception.

"Yeah," Marcus answered.

"Where ya' at?"

"Jus' leavin' the hospital boutta' go get me some sleep."

"How she doin'?" Steve asked, showing concern for his mother-in-law.

"She was sleep when I left. The doctors took her to that bullshit treatment." Marcus wasn't convinced that the chemotherapy or radiology treatments were good options for helping his grandmother. He craved to find a better solution, but at this point options were limited.

"Was Chris up there?" Steve asked.

"Naw."

"I told him to take his ass up to that hospital this morning. He stayed out all night laid up wit'

211

that lil girl. Now he act like he don't wanna answer his damn phone."

"What happened at the game?"

"You must ain't read the papers. That lil nigga showed out! That's all everybody in the neighborhood been talkin' 'bout."

"Straight up!" Marcus forced out his excitement.

"Aey, I'm sitting over here at the old house right now having a drank, why don't you come through? I been meaning to holla' at'chu 'bout some'nt anyway."

"Man, can it wait? I'm tired as hell."

"Really it can't. I 'posed to been ran this across to you."

"A'ight, I'a be through there in about ten minutes."

Since Steve wanted to see him so urgently, the matter had to be important. So he made his way towards the house on 19th and Hamlin. Marcus allowed Steve and a couple others to have access to the remodeled single family home in case of any emergencies.

After driving for all of ten minutes, Marcus pulled in the back alley and called Steve's phone. Steve was already standing at the back door waiting, on point as usual. After making it in the house Marcus staggered his way to the nearest couch without even bothering to take off his leather jacket. From the look of things Steve was spending his alone time meditating through deep thoughts. He had

212

Sports Center on the big screen with a half-empty fifth of Tanqueray and a Mr. Pure orange juice resting on the coffee table right next to a Chicago Sun-Times newspaper. Steve trailed behind Marcus to the front room and slumped down into the loveseat directly across from him. He then grabbed the newspaper off the table and tossed it on Marcus's lap.

"Check out the high school basketball section," he insisted.

Marcus turned straight to the section. In big bold letters, the heading read "THE WESTINGHOUSE Warriors SUPERSTAR PLAYER HAS THE BREAK OUT GAME OF HIS CAREER SCORING AN AMAZING 61 POINTS!" The way that Marcus jumped from his seat you could hardly tell he was exhausted.

"Get the fuck outta' here! He did 'em like that?"

Steve smiled at Marcus reaction then told him, "That's jus' half of it. Keep reading."

Marcus stood there and read the remainder of the article, which was solely about Chris' heroic championship performance. The article mentioned everything from the games play-by-play action all the way down to scouts talking about getting Chris to commit a year early to their programs. Marcus got to the section where Chris was being interviewed. After reading his brother's sentimental dedication to their grandmother, he simply smiled and then immediately began dialing numbers on his cell.

"I been callin 'em all morning. Maybe he'll answer for you." Steve said as he sipped on his glass of Tang.

After three unsuccessful attempts, Marcus left a message on his voice mail.

"Awe, you too important to answer my calls now, huh?!" He laughed cheerfully. "That's a'ight, I'a catch up wit'chu later." Marcus ended the call and got play-by-play details on the game from Steve.

After 10 minutes of praising Chris' basketball skills Steve switched to the more risky subject that had been haunting his mind. As they continued to ramble on about Chris' game Marcus sat back down and became more comfortable, he even poured himself a glass of Tang and orange juice. No matter how comfortable he got nothing could've prepared him for the news that was about to be laid on him.

"Yeah man, I been lying low lately tryna' figure some shit out," Steve said with a more serious approach.

"Big C claimed you ain't been fuckin' wit'em lately, wassup wit' that?"

Taking a sip from his glass, Steve gave Marcus a belligerent look and said, "He ain't heard from me 'cause that's who I been checkin' up on."

Little did Steve know, Marcus was having major concerns himself about the long lived Chief. Instead of speaking on it, he let Steve continue.

"Since reading that letter, I took it upon myself to do some investigating. I guess it's true what they say... when you go searching you find what the hell you lookin' for."

Marcus's attention grew profoundly as he anticipated on what was to be said next. Steve paused before speaking again causing Marcus to show a rare sign of impatience. He eagerly wanted to see if his intuition was guiding him correctly.

"So what'chu sayin'?!" Marcus asked slightly irritably.

Staring into space with a disappointed expression Steve replied, "The person I dedicated half my fuckin' life to ain't been righteous." He took another sip from his glass and continued, "I caught 'em leavin' a meeting with that crooked mothafucka Alderman Davis and to make shit worst they was there with the devil himself."

"The devil himself?" Marcus stood up and questioned suspiciously. "Who you talkin' 'bout?!"

Before answering, Steve gulped the remainder of his drink, slammed the empty glass down on the coffee table, and dreadfully replied, "Chronin!"

Marcus's jaw dropped after hearing the detective's name mentioned. The past events immediately played back in Marcus memory bank.

That explains every thang... All he could envision was detective Chronin driving down 21st looking at him with a certain glare and Big C blatantly lying to his face about not having any dealings with the slimy detective. At that very moment, Marcus felt the ultimate betrayal.

Watching Marcus pace back and forth with his mind wondering, Steve knew he hadn't told him the half of Big C wrongdoings. Afraid of how Marcus would react to the rest of the news, Steve hesitated before saying, "Marcus, I think you need to sit down."

"Fuck I need to sit down for," he snapped. "You the reason the shit got this far! I 'posed to been whacked his ass when I first got word he was workin' wit' 'dem people!"

"First of all, you gettin' way too excited for me. You need to calm your nerves and listen to what else I gotta' tell you!"

Marcus reluctantly sat down and faced Steve, showing an insidious mug.

"C recently mentioned some shit to me that I swear I knew nuttin' about."

"What, that he been a fuckin' stool pigeon all this time?" Marcus's assumption came out sarcastically.

"Nah," Steve replied with all seriousness. "After all these years this nigga jus' recently came out and admitted that--that he was the--the trigga man behind ya' Pops murder."

Steve knew after releasing that statement he had declared war. At this point, it did not matter. He had already made up his mind that Big C had to pay for disrespecting the Nation. Marcus, on the other hand, had developed a more personal vendetta. Steve expected Marcus to lash out from the news, but instead he sat there in complete silence, which was even more dangerous. Marcus's murderous expression spoke volumes and Steve was trying to find the words to calm the situation.

"Now, look Marcus, I know what'chu thinkin' right now. But we gotta keep a cool head and do things right." Steve knew that assassinating a mob figure like Big C had to be done in a clever fashion. Marcus kept silent while Steve spoke on a resolution. "I'm asking you, naw fuck 'dat, I'm begging you not to go do some'nt crazy that could get us all killed. Please, let me handle this shit. I promise you, he won't know what hit 'em."

"Let'chu handle it?!" Marcus yelled emotionally. "I been lettin' you handle shit for years and look where it got me!" He exclaimed, giving Steve a hurt and disgusted look. After a couple seconds of a silent stare off, Marcus stood to his feet and stormed towards the back door with his mind set on kill mode.

Before Marcus could make it to the back door Steve yelled out, "Marcus! I got this!" Marcus never broke stride. The only reply Steve got was the sounds of his tires burning rubber. Steve knew then that Marcus had turned into a walking time bomb and it was little he could do or say to stop him!

Later that evening an unexpected call from Rico rescinded Marcus's thoughts of getting some well-needed rest and making it back to the hospital. Marcus mind was still distraught from how he'd been bamboozled for so many years. He immediately began plotting once leaving Steve's presence. There was no way he could allow Big C to continue breathing after finding out he was the reason a very important part of him was dead. Marcus's route to the hospital was detoured due to the fact that Rico claimed he had money that was owed to him from other high ranked officials. Marcus pulled into a BP gas station in a neutral area downtown and waited patiently on Rico to pull up. Usually, Marcus would send one of his personal guys to pick up petty cash, but because he hadn't been around lately, Rico insisted on seeing him. He waited about ten minutes before Rico speedily pulled in right beside Marcus in his Lexus coupe. He briskly hopped out in his normal arrogant demeanor and approached the truck.

"Wassup fool," he greeted excitedly while settling inside Marcus's ride. "You been missing in action lately, ain'tchu... I been blowin' yo' phone up."

Not matching his energy, Marcus lowly replied, "I been watchin' over my gran'ma. She in the hospital wit' lung cancer."

"What...!" Rico said with an act of sincerity. "Man, I'm sorry to hear that, Lord. I'ma make sure I keep her in my prayers."

Even though Rico was a brother of the Nation, Marcus ignored his condolences knowing his heart was cold as ice and had no genuine feelings. Seconds later, Rico went straight to street business. He reached down in his crotch area and pulled out a small brown paper bag with four neatly folded, thick rubber banded stacks. In the midst of informing Marcus on existing problems inside the mob, Rico strangely brought up a couple topics that Marcus had no interest in talking about at that moment.

"You been keepin' up wit' Smitty? How Chief doin', man?"

Before answering, Marcus looked at him confusedly then said, "Every thang good. I make sho' him and his family ain't wantin' for nuttin'."

"I'm surprised he ain't sent word to the streets tryna' give orders on how to handle shit out here. You know how he do," Rico stated, but failed to get a response from Marcus. Noticing how Marcus was contemplating on certain thoughts, Rico prepared for an exit. "Well, I ain't gon' hold you up, I kno' you a busy man and everything. I jus' wanted to drop off the rest of that change I owed you." They shook up with each other and Rico reached for the door handle. Right before opening the door, he stalled up and mentioned, "Awe yeah, you ain't tell me yo' lil brotha' around this bitch ballin' like he Jordan-n-shit. Lil dude putting up 60 on niggas, huh! I see he the talk of the city!"

"Yeah, he be doin' his thang," Marcus responded, cracking a half smile.

"Make sho' he stay on it. I'a love to see one of our lil Lords in the NBA representin'. Hey, you never know, right?" He said with a roguish look while stepping out the truck. Before shutting the door Rico quoted, "If you need me for anything, I mean anything; don't hesitate to hit my phone, a'ight." Marcus simply gave a nod and they went their separate ways. Marcus continued to go on about his business without giving a second thought to the meeting with Rico. All his mind could ponder was murderous thoughts. His appetite for destruction had grown enormously and Big C was his main course.

Fifteen minutes into driving on the 290 West expressway, Marcus had decided to camp out at one of his rarely used apartments in Hillside, a small suburb minutes from the inner city. Just as he prepared to ease his mind and think more clearly on his next move a call came through. Looking down at the caller ID, he smiled as he recognized the number.

"Awe, now you wanna call," he answered lightheartedly, "What, you think you too special to answer ya' phone 'cause you dropped 61 and yo' name ringing all around the city-n-shit!" Marcus laughed out, anticipating a typical cocky response from his young superstar brother.

"Naw mothafucka! I ain't special, but this lil nigga we got might be!" The ghastly, intimidating voice on the other end grumbled out.

"What! Man who the fuck is this?" Marcus said while looking into the phone thinking a prank was being played on him.

"Big bra, I need you, man!!! I need you!!!" Chris' panicky voice cried out through the receiver in pure desperation.

"Chris...?! Chris!!"

"Now think we playin' if you want to, yo' momma gon' be seeing her baby on the 10 o'clock news and it won't be for scoring 60 points, nigga!"

Recklessly exiting off at the Wolf Road ramp, Marcus quickly pulled over at the nearest parking lot insight.

"Whoeva' this is, I hope you kno' what the fuck you gettin' yo'self into!" Marcus retorted dangerously with his words coming through clenched teeth.

"A gun to ya' lil brotha' face and that's all you could come up wit'?! Look, when I call back hopefully you be ready to talk wit' some sense, if not, consider this lil mothafucka DOA!"

"Listen here," Marcus got ready to respond. "Hello, hello...!" He looked down at the phone and the call had ended. "Fuck!!!" Marcus dialed the number back several timesto no avail. With tears of anger forming in his eyes, he flung his Nextel aside and began beating on the steering wheel relentlessly out of fear of something gruesome happening to Chris.

36

"How are you feeling today, beautiful?" Sylvia asked while standing over her ailing mother in the hospital room. Grandma Emma was responsive, but the chemotherapy sessions had weakened her. "I want to show you what your grandson did." Sylvia happily said as she brought out the newspaper articles. Showing Grandma Emma the picture of Chris being held up by his team and reading the passage where he dedicated his historic point total to his grandmother seemed to have uplifted her spirits. She had been one of Chris's biggest fans ever since he first picked up a basketball.

After seeing the newspaper article Grandma Emma painfully uttered, "Well, where is my baby? I know I haven't seen him in a couple days."

"Momma, you know how teenagers are these days. They get older and start feeling themselves. I'm sure he'll make his way up here tomorrow. You just get some rest and don't worry about nothing."

Chris never came home and even though it hadn't been a full 24 hours Sylvia had begun to worry about Chris, but her primary concern was helping her mother. She didn't allow any other situations outside of that to worry her at the moment.

The chemo sessions were breaking Grandma Emma down and it was becoming noticeable. She was barely walking on her own and her appetite had vastly declined. Solid foods were no longer in her diet, only Ensure nutrient supplements and unseasoned hospital food. Her had hair started thinning out in certain areas. Her condition wasn't panning out how the family had hoped. It seemed everyone was merely going through the motions, preparing themselves for the worst.

During most of Sylvia's stay at the hospital she tried to make every moment joyful. Often times they reminisced on past memories. Although the joy was temporary, at times it prevented the tears.

Sitting at the edge of the bed staring into space Sylvia began to speak out reflectively.

"As long as I could remember, you have always been the spiritual backbone to our family," Sylvia said in a mesmerizing fashion as she began caressing her mother's feet. "I will never forget the scripture you use to recite every time things got tough for me... 'Weeping may endure for a night, but joy comes in the morning'."

Grandma Emma gave off an assuring nod and gentle smile towards the scripture verse. Sylvia couldn't hold back the tears as she continued on, "Momma without you helping me raise them boys, I don't know how I would've did it. I love you so much..." Sylvia scooted up towards the head of the bed and they both gazed lovingly into each other's teary eyes. Taking hold of her daughter's hand, Grandma Emma managed to mutter out, "I love you too, shuga. I love all y'all. I really don't feel like the Lord is through using me. I still have a lot of work to do."

"That's why we need for you to be strong, Momma. Don't give up on us. As long as we keep our faith in God, He'll handle the rest."

For the remainder of her stay at the hospital, Sylvia simply enjoyed her mother's presence and did everything in her power to keep their minds off the situation. Although in the back of her mind, she was thinking of other ways to help treat her mother's condition. It seemed that the doctors had given up on the fight against the cancer. Instead, their minds were stuck on the three-month prognosis that Sylvia and the Williams family highly resented.

Chapter
37

Upon returning to the West Side, Marcus frantically called Steve and his personal guys and explained the critical situation involving Chris. The basement of the house on 19th and Hamlin was the meeting spot. The basement wasn't nearly a livable space. It was only used as a storage space for weapons of mass destruction. All artillery that was meant for street warfare was in the basement. There were barrels filled with all sorts of handguns, semi-autos, and fully-autos. Marcus even had a few hand grenades and several Kevlar and Teflon vests in his arsenal.

The six of them stood within the sewage scented, mildew stained walls contemplating on whom to bring the wrath down on. Most of the basement was pitch black except for the spots where a few flimsy hanging light bulbs were stationed. Hours had passed since the disturbing call came through from the perpetrators. Marcus kept calling Chris' phone from different numbers, but the voicemail was the only answer he got. Everyone was uptight and showing their frustrations except Steve. His silence and stone cold expression defined the seriousness of the situation.

"You think it was them 'Breeds?" Peewee asked vigorously. "I'll fuckin' kill 'dem niggaz, whether it was them or not. You jus' tell me to. Give the word Chief, jus' give the word."

Lil G gestured with both hands, his every movement showing in shadows on the wall, pleading, "What'chu want us to do Chief? The brothas jus' waitin' for the word. We cain't jus' sit here and—"

"Gettin' me, I understand," Marcus contemplated in a daze after cutting Lil G's statement short. "But Chris? Who did Chris ever hurt? And who don't like Chris? Everybody likes Chris..."

Marcus was trying to find a logical explanation for his brothers kidnapping. He couldn't figure out who would want to hurt Chris, being that he was a known high school basketball star. To make matters worse, there were no dangerous wars in progress involving Marcus and his mob so he didn't feel the need to prevent Chris from riding through certain 'hoods. Despite not having any known street problems, Marcus's success as a Chief made anyone close to him subject to danger at any given time.

With a look of affliction, Steve finally broke his silence. In the midst of clips being inserted and the sounds of guns clacking he said, "It could've been anybody..." He speculated on the possibilities. "A gaddamn fiend. Or a business rival. Or some dumb-ass niggaz tryna' make a name... Or maybe even one of our own people we neglected without realizing it..."

Steve directed his last statement towards Marcus while gaining everyone else's attention as they began to think more deeply on the possibilities. Marcus's personal crew was in the blind on the situation concerning Big C and Smitty. At this point, they didn't know what to think and only hoped for a call to come through so that they could compromise with the kidnappers and hopefully spare Chris' life.

"Whateva' the case may be; I need my son back in one piece without the police gettin' involved. He don't need to be in the news for some shit like this after that big game he jus' had. So as long as we can help it, keep my wife from finding out," Steve spoke in a menacing tone. "I'm gon' get my boy back, no matter the cost!"

Strapping on bulletproof vests, they all began tucking pistols of their choice. Marlin, Peewee, Lil G, and J.R. all loaded the street sweepers to supply the soldiers they had handpicked to ride out. Marcus had holsters for his chrome twin double 45s with silencers and hollow tip bullets. Steve, on the other hand carried a couple of 9mm Rugers. Everyone had on the proper attire for situations like this: All black everything, with leather gloves and ski masks.

As Marcus was instructing his team and giving them their posts, his phone began to ring. He unclipped the Nextel from his waistline and looked down at the phone and over at Steve and said, "It's a private number." Everyone glanced around at each other as Steve head signaled Marcus to answer. Marcus pressed send and put the phone on speaker. Before he could answer, a growling voice came stumbling through the receiver.

"I hope you what'nt stupid enough to get them people involved... Nah, not you, you'a gangsta', you should know better."

"Where the fuck my brotha' at, man?!" Marcus said, exposing fumes through his tone.

"Chill homey, he ain't dead... yet. The choices you make will determine 'dat."

"Marcus please give 'em what they want, bruh! They gone kill me!" Chris's perturbed voice came storming through the phone. Before he was able to say anything else, his words became muffled.

After hearing Chris's voice and imagining the torture that he could be enduring, all the body language and facial expressions in the basement were heart wrenching. The tension in the air was thick.

"Now you wanna talk bin'nis or you wanna keep bullshittin'?!" the perp exclaimed.

Marcus glanced around and peeped the distress in Steve's face before calmly replying, "Whateva' you want, jus' don't hurt 'em..."

"Well since we is dealing wit'a young superstar I figure he gotta' be worth a lil some'nt to you and we all kno' money ain't a thang to you. So I say a light... five hunit', thousand that is. I kno' that's chump change to you."

Marcus became silent and simply shook his head at the ransom that was forced upon him. He never saw it coming and at this point, he felt helpless and defeated. No power or money could compensate for his brother's life. True enough, the money wasn't the issue, but having to give it up forcibly was the hard pill to swallow. Marcus knew situations like this were bound to happen eventually, but never in a thousand years did he imagine it to hit so close to home.

After about ten seconds of silence on the phone, the caller blurted out. "I kno' it's a lot to think about, so we'll give you some time," he stated sarcastically. "But remember, our patience is running real thin and if I'm not mistaken, ya' boy here got some pretty important games coming up. If he's a no-show, that could bring a lot of unwanted attention. Please believe me; the results won't be good if that happens..."

With that said, the call ended leaving everyone in dismay. They knew there was no way around paying the ransom, no matter what the amount was. Marcus had money put up for street emergencies like these, but never did he think it would have to come into play for Chris. At this point, the ball was in the perp's court and Marcus had to abide by their commands. Luckily, the ransom amount was reachable, making it possible for him to pay for his brother's life. But it didn't stop the raging fire from burning him up inside.

Marcus had all his guys positioned for what was to come. He sent J.R. to gather the ransom money and kept him on standby until it was time to deliver. A considerable amount of time had passed since the first call came in from the kidnappers and it was now going into late morning hours. Five carloads of Lords parked along the block of 19th and Hamlin ready to assist Marcus and Steve as they sat alone in a low-key unrecognizable car.

With a blank expression Steve meekly spat out, "You been way too good to these niggaz..." He continued on to say, "These last few years, you been consistently putting out the best dope this city seen in a long time. 'Cause of you, a lot of mothafuckas done got rich out here on these streets..."

"I been doin' ery'thing I 'posed to do. Lockin' down the areas that belong to me and makin' sure every righteous Vice Lord brotha' get their proper share," Marcus confusedly responded.

"Yeah that's true, but it comes a time when you have to fall back and let niggaz find their own way. You are becoming too powerful and that alone makes you a target. Not jus' with the law or some unknown enemies, but also within the Nation."

"So what'chu sayin', me handlin' bin'nis the right way got Chris snatched up? Or me handlin' bin'nis made YOUR Chief turn into a secret informant?!" Marcus shot back fiercely.

"Nawl, but what I am sayin' is," Steve retorted arguably, "...you need to dry the land up for a while and make these mothafuckas find they own way.

Listen man, if you ain't rich by now, then you never gonna be. Quit makin' a career out of this shit and get the fuck out while you still alive! Twenty years of me being in these streets I have yet seen a'mafucka retire on top!"

Steve's statement had Marcus momentarily speechless. Over the course of his five year run as a Chief, he became a multi-millionaire. In spite of being shot up and losing a best friend to gun violence the streets had been good to him. He never stepped foot inside of a penitentiary and had no pending cases. Marcus was accustomed to dealing with critical situations concerning his mob, but Chris' kidnapping imposed a much more endearing threat.

Silently rambling through frustrating thoughts the ring they were eagerly waiting on brought them to attention.

"I got what'chu want, now name the spot!" Marcus voice stormed through the receiver as he answered already knowing the private number was from the perps.

"On 115th and Halsted in the alley behind the McDonald's. Drop it in the large dumpster."

"How I 'posed to kno' he still in one piece right now!" Marcus's blood was boiling. There was nothing he wanted more than to take the breath out of the person on the other end and whoever else was behind the ransom demands.

"Chill, we takin' good care of'em..." the caller assured, "...aey, take that shit off his mouth and

Michael F. Blake

make 'em talk..." Chris forced out a few mumbled words assuring that he was still alive and conscious. Marcus vengefully said, "Listen, if it's somethin' as small as a scratch on my brotha'... I swear fo' God Imma hunt you mothafuckas down 'til my dyin' day! You understand what the fuck I'm tellin' you?" The only reply Marcus got was the dial tone. The intense level grew to an all-time high. Marcus realized how risky it was dropping off such a large amount of cash in an unfamiliar spot only to hope they come through on their end. At this point his choices were limited, but the chance they were taking was well worth getting Chris back alive and in one piece.

After hanging up Marcus quickly called J.R. to meet him back on the block. Within ten minutes he was pulling up with two large army fatigue duffle bags filled with large bills. Every bit of the $500,000 was in the bag. Marcus let everyone know the destination as they began clearing off 19th. The scene as they left the block was similar to how the Secret Service protects the President with cars in the front and back of Marcus. They drove in an orderly fashion on their way to the Wild Hunits.

Chapter 38

Marcus and the slew of cars that followed got off the Bishop Ford expressway and made a quick right on 115th Street. As they cruised down 115th, the silence in the car explained the intensity that was in the air. Who the hell would come all the way out here? The only person came to mind was Rico, but he quickly erased the vague thought.

Cautiously pulling up in an alley behind McDonald's, Marcus made a phone call to J.R. instructing him on where to make the drop off. J.R., accompanied by a couple of soldiers, carried the two hefty duffle bags over to a large dumpster. After the drop off, Marcus and his crew eased off into the gloomy, light drizzling rain drops, feeling more vulnerable than ever before.

After leaving the drop off spot, a private call came through. Marcus was agitated with the cat and mouse game the kidnappers were playing.

"You got what'chu wanted. Now where the fuck is my brotha'?!" Marcus angrily spoke through the receiver with Steve watching his every move.

"I see you follow instructions well," the perp sarcastically replied.

"Fuck all 'dat! Where my brotha' at!"

"Uhmmmm, let me think..." The caller chuckled before finishing his statement, "Calm ya' nerves homey. You can find the 'lil nigga on Chicago Avenue and Austin in the back of the alley."

Marcus quickly ended the call and led the way to the very familiar street with five car loads of Lords trailing behind him. Marcus speedily swerved from lane to lane on the expressway heading back towards the West Side. The reckless driving continued after exiting the expressway in route to their destination.

Arriving to the area, Marcus and his crew scoured several pitch black alleys, still no Chris. Just when Marcus thought he was about to explode, he glanced in his rearview mirror and noticed one of the trailing vehicles slowing down. He brought his car to a complete stop immediately. He jumped out frantically running toward his guys who signaled him to stop. As he drew closer to the abandoned garage, he recognized a body inside struggling to sit upright. He had a pillow case wrapped around his head and his hands were tied behind his back.

"Chris! Chris! You okay!" He hollered as he snatched the tightly wrapped pillow case from Chris's head, only to find his mouth duck taped.

"Man, son I thought we'd never see your face again!" An emotional Steve shouted out as he ran up to console his son.

As tears flowed down a wide-eyed Chris's face, the muffled cries expressed his overwhelming joy of being found alive. After ripping the grey tape from his mouth and untying his arms, Marcus and Steve examined Chris for any physical damage while interrogating his memory bank. A badly traumatized Chris attempted to talk but raw emotions took over as they escorted him to the car.

Looking back at his terribly shaken younger brother, Marcus gazed into his eyes and made a heartfelt vow.

"I swear to God if I don't do nothing else, I promise you I'm gon' find the mothafuckas who behind this shit!"

Marcus led the way as they all vanished into the foggy night. Steve sat on the passenger side in his signature silent mode. The deep thoughts couldn't possibly be good for the other side.

39

On an unseasonably warm morning in October, Big C pulled up to Castle Car Wash in his antique Rolls Royce. The neighborhood car wash located on 16th was one of several businesses that Big C had ties with. Before fully stepping out of the car, Big C was surrounded by a couple of car wash attendants and a few of his local soldiers. Big C strolled through the car wash briefly conversing with the hands-on owners as he headed towards a private office space in the back.

Moments later another vehicle pulled up. Marcus hopped out of the passenger seat before Marlin could completely park. By his demeanor and the bag strapped on his shoulder, you could tell he was there for nothing else other than business. Marcus's brisk walk through the car wash was slightly different than Big C's. Instead of talking he simply gave off nods to all the acknowledgements that came his way.

Before walking into the office Marcus was met
by a familiar face that stood on security. The
murderous mean mug Marcus had on his face spoke
volumes and was enough to let the security know to
step out of the way. Being in the presence of Big C
for the first time since receiving the news that he was
the man who murdered his father electrified Marcus
with a bundle of emotions that was eating him alive
inside. Standing there with the gym bag across his
shoulders, his beady eyes and strong clinched jaws
showed the newly built hatred being held back.
Marcus knew if he had openly expressed his anger it
would have been a definite suicide mission.

"Okay ... I'ma get witcha' in a minute" Big C
ended his call as he stepped closer to Marcus to
greet him. "Marcus, how you feeling brotha?" Big C
asked as they shook up and shoulder dapped each
other.

"Ery'thing aw'right Chief."

Big C took a step back and looked Marcus
square in the eyes. He could see the obvious distress
on Marcus's face and assumed the cause of it was
from Chris kidnapping.

"How ya' lil' brotha coming along?

Marcus simply gave him a nod before handing
over the bag. After checking inside and seeing the
neat money stacks, Big C proceeded to prolong the
unwanted conversation. "You know, if it was more
loyal mothafuckas out here like us that respected the
game, we wouldn't have to worry about the bullshit."

Marcus immediately had a disturbing image of his father being murdered by the person standing directly in front of him. Having to blink several times to snap out of a troubling trance, Marcus made an attempt to exit Big C's presence before these strong emotions took control.

"Chief look, I jus came to drop that package off to you. I really need to get outta here. I got some shit I need to handle."

"Okay, okay, I ain't gon' hold you up. I jus' want you to kno' one thing before you leave... I gotcha back. And you best believe that situation gon' get handled." Big C said with his most sincere look.

Marcus gave him a wink and showed a slight smirk before muttering out, "Awe, I know." Marcus turned toward the door, leaving Big C in a puzzling daze. His attention quickly switched over to the money that was delivered to him as he flicked a thick rubber band stack in the air while sporting a huge smile.

Thirty minutes later, as he was on his way out of the car wash with his security trailing behind toting the sack of money, Big C stopped to converse with a few business associates. During their conversation a female with a strange walk strolled up into the lobby and kindly interrupted the conversation. "Excuse me, are you guys open?" One of the car wash workers greeted her and directed the woman to the entrance. Big C and his comrades continued talking. The woman wore baggy clothes, dark shades, and a long jet black wig that nearly covered her entire face giving Big C and his guys no reason to stare her down.

The woman turned towards the group with one hand in her shoulder strapped purse and said, "Awe, one more thing."

In what seemed like slow motion, the woman revealed a hand sized, double barrel 32 revolver with a pearl white handle and aimed it at the back of Big C's head. While the others scrambled for cover, Big C never had a chance as the single shot pierced viciously through the back of his head. The tall, slender woman jetted off like a seasoned athlete, leaving behind a distraught group and a long lived Chief lying face down in a pool of his own blood.

Epilogue

The grey and rainy morning was a perfect setting as Marcus and Steve sat next to each other in the front pews inside Corbin's Funeral Home on Madison. The funeral was standing room only and looked more like a popular hood night club than a funeral for a long lived Chief. As the preacher spoke what most thought was jive, Marcus and Steve listened with blank expressions as security surrounded them like the Secret Service protecting the President.

Being so close to the 24 karat gold, glass protected casket, Marcus and Steve were able to clearly see all passing mourners and their reactions. They witnessed everything from longtime leaders of other branches paying their respect, to others showing their explicit disgust. They even saw Chronin walk up to view the street legend's corpse. Only his view wasn't meant for mourning. He looked as though he was angered at the fact that Big C died before he had a chance to add him to the long list of reigning Chiefs that he had personally brought down.

Walking out of the funeral home doors with security on their heels, Marcus and Steve briefly spoke and shook up with hundreds of different VL members, some old school, some street soldiers. Marcus and Steve were able to step aside from all the emotional commotion that stood outside of the funeral home. Still in a state of shock with a million and one thoughts rambling through his mind, Marcus looked over at Steve and said, "What bitch would have the balls to run up in the car wash on Chief like 'dat? And not only that, she beat me to it." Marcus spoke in a confused low pitched tone that only Steve could hear.

Steve gazed into Marcus's eyes with a sarcastic grin and simply said, "You kno', I gained a new found respect for women in heels. It's much harder than it looks." Steve said with a slight chuckle as he winked at Marcus.

Marcus took a step back, mouth wide open and eyes bucked looking in total disbelief and said, "Damn Pops, say it ain't so..."

THE SAGA CONTINUES WITH
"The Holy City III: Legit Hustlin'"

Michael F. Blake

WE ARE TEAM DELPHINE

Follow us on Instagram and Twitter
@DelphinePub
FaceBook: DelphinePublications

Join our newsletter by texting your email to
678 871-7157

Also in Stores

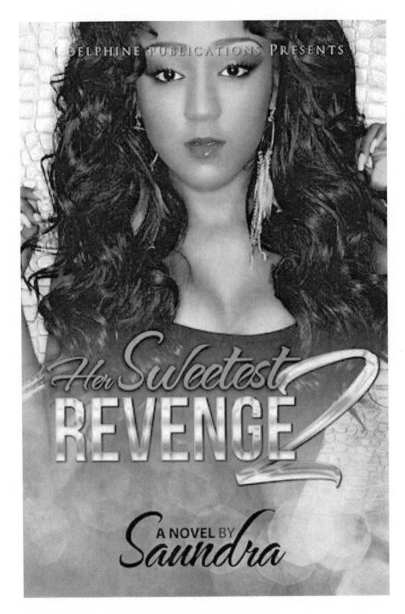

{ DELPHINE PUBLICATIONS PRESENTS }

Bitter Taste
OF
LOVE

STACEY COVINGTON-LEE

AUTHOR OF *THE KNIFE IN MY BACK*

{ DELPHINE PUBLICATIONS PRESENTS }

Lies
UNLEASHED
II

A Novel By
TAMMARA MATTHEWS

CPSIA information can be obtained at www.ICGtesting.com
Printed in the USA
LVOW13s1554291013

359124LV00001B/293/P